THE SWEETEST KISS

THE SWEETEST KISS

RAVISHING VAMPIRE EROTICA

EDITED BY
D. L. KING

CLEIS
PRESS

Published in the United States by Cleis Press Inc., P.O. Box 14697, San Francisco, California 94114.

Printed in Canada.
Cover design: Scott Idleman
Cover photograph: Karen Moskowitz/Getty Images
Text design: Frank Wiedemann
Cleis Press logo art: Juana Alicia
First Edition.
10 9 8 7 6 5 4 3 2 1

ISBN: 978-1-57344-371-5

"Red by Any Other Name," by Kathleen Bradean, previously appeared in *Blood Surrender* (Blue Moon, 2005).

Contents

MIDNIGHT AT SHEREMETYEVO

Remittance Girl

They say that rules are made to be broken, but "they" haven't met Daniel. He takes rules very seriously because, he insists, they keep us alive. This is something of a problematic statement, but to dwell on technicalities would be a grave mistake. Mistakes get you a month in a four-by-four cell, a hundred feet below the rumbling streets of Mumbai with no air, no light, no food and a great deal of time to think.

Ever since I joined the family, the annual journey to Zürich to arrange our legal and financial affairs has fallen to me. I'm the only one of us left who still loves the cold, the only one who yearns for a nice crisp snowy night. I go because I'm clever with numbers and patient with the men in the suits. Daniel says their plump, moist bankers' hands make him want to rip their throats out. Most of all, I get to go because I'm the reliable one: Marta the obedient, Marta the sensible; Marta, Daniel's pet. Usually.

I have twenty-two days left to stew in this infernal hole—a lot of time to contemplate my transgression. Between the occasional visits of hapless cockroaches, I remember the taste of him, the burning flood of his young life as it surged into my mouth. I picture the mothlike fluttering of his pale eyelids just before the end. The haunting, reverberating gasps of his pent-up desire are so loud in my head; sometimes I think it will drive me insane. But I tell myself the story over and over again, if only to keep my mind off the time.

My February visit to the head office of Credit Suisse had passed with the same gratifying efficiency as always. The family banks there because Daniel knew Auguste Escher, the founder's wife, rather intimately. Both the history and the irony of this escapes me. Still, the stability of the Swiss franc on long-term deposit is nothing to be sniffed at. I dealt, as always, with Herr Rohner. We discussed dispositions and made a few changes to our investment strategy and I finished my business on a beautifully snowy Thursday evening.

There were no direct night flights back to Mumbai, so I settled for what I could get: a late Aeroflot charter with a short transfer in Moscow. I landed at Sheremetyevo International at eleven thirty.

Perhaps it was the marbled, morguelike stillness of the place, or because I hadn't fed for more than three days. Maybe it was the fact that my body clock was so confused from all the traveling, but for some reason, I was feeling a little vulnerable. And he looked so innocent, so scrumptious—like a little lost piece of patisserie—alert and slightly out of place in that huge, cold mausoleum of an airport.

The transit lounge was almost empty. The polished granite hall with its floor-to-ceiling windows looking out onto a dark and frost-carpeted runway was hardly conducive to lounging. Neither were the hard, mean, plastic-molded seats in dull 1970s burnt orange.

At the far end, by the entrance to the washrooms, a trio of

corpulent Russian matrons in dusty navy blue uniforms with tarnished brass buttons gossiped percussively. I had met them earlier, looking for directions to the gate. They had bristled and clucked at me indecipherably, making broad shooing gestures with their meaty red hands. Their enormous bosoms had heaved and strained in communal, unfathomable indignation and they had smelled of boiled cabbage. Now they were back at it, discussing something scandalous and noteworthy.

I guessed the boy to be no more than twenty-five. After a few minutes of pacing aimlessly along the line of windows, he took a seat opposite mine in the empty concourse. His silvery, ash-blond hair was cut so short it looked like a mousy velvet cap over his beautifully sculpted head. The dull lights in the ceiling picked up the tips of individual strands, making them shimmer as if he were a sweet Nordic angel. And his lips, full, sensuous and cherubic, were so plump it looked like he had a hard time keeping them closed. He wetted them nervously with an agile pink tongue as he glanced about. People who disdain the flesh have never seen that boy's lips.

Occasionally, unintelligible announcements reverberated around the hollow room from a dilapidated public address system recessed into the vaulted ceiling. When they did, the boy would look up at the speakers, as if he stood a better chance of understanding what was being said by staring at the source of the sound. His long, sinuous neck stretched upward, showing faint blue veins under his almost translucent skin. The movement accentuated his delicately carved Adam's apple. I toyed with biblical analogies of forbidden fruit before forcing myself to look away.

He gnawed at his lower lip and sucked it petulantly into his mouth. Mine watered and I must have swallowed rather loudly, because he looked at me and offered a nervous smile. I didn't return it. Instead I reminded myself of the rules: no playing away from home base, no damage to civilians, no indulging in risky behavior, and—most of all—no corrupting youth; all the good, sensible rules that kept me safe. That kept us all safe.

He must have felt that I was the only friendly face he was likely to see for the next few hours—not that my face is particularly friendly. Tall and gaunt, alabaster pale and dark haired, I'm not all that approachable. Daniel says I have a classic elegance, but most men look from a distance and give me a wide berth.

But this boy—this silly, silly boy—decided that, at midnight and far from home, I was companionship. He pushed himself lithely out of his seat, leaving his knapsack where it lay, and walked over to me.

"Do you speak English?"

Oh, he was lovely! His coltish frame stood at a polite distance, skittish and fine boned. "Yes, I do."

The boy beamed in triumph and gestured to the seat beside mine. "Do you mind if I sit?"

I glanced from the boy to the seat adjoining mine and back up at him. At that moment I could have done the right thing. I could have—should have—cold-shouldered him, but I didn't. "No. Please do."

As he sat down, I caught scent of him; it was enough to make angels drool: sweet, clean, young skin with a tickle of salt and the tang of a recent bout of masturbation. It was almost unbearable as his shoulder brushed mine. He turned in his seat to face me.

"Where are you going, if I might ask?"

To hell, you foolish boy, I almost replied. "To Mumbai."

He grinned broadly, nodded his head, and pointed to his backpack. "Me too! I go traveling, to see India." Then he tilted his head and appraised me in that overt way that only the pain-fully young manage to get away with. "But why do you choose to go by Aeroflot? Not such a nice airline but cheap. You do not look like you need to fly cheap."

No. I was stinking rich and old enough to be his great grand-mother. "It's the only night flight," I replied, and caught myself staring directly into his eyes. His lashes were dense dark fringes. The overheads struck them and cast them in lacy shadows against his cheeks.

For a moment he did nothing. Perhaps my eyes had stunned him; they do that sometimes—black rings surrounding indigo and ultramarine irises, shot through with topaz. I blinked to release him.

He blinked back a couple of times and continued with his beautifully accented traveler's banter. "I am from Denmark… and you?"

Oh yes, I could have still been good and decent and kind, but hunger was gnawing at my muscles and the scent of him ate tiny holes though my skin. I was feeling so weak and he was so exquisite. I reached over, placed my hand upon his knee and laughed softly.

"I'm from many places. But now I live in India."

The boy began jabbering away about the subcontinent and all the mysteries it held. He spoke excitedly. He gazed out over the dark runway one moment and then deep into my eyes the next. All that energy flowed through me like clear, crisp water. What would it be like to feel so young again? To see the world with new, eager eyes? My jaw ached. Beneath my tongue the saliva surged and I swallowed it down, along with the guilt that rose like bile in my throat.

His voice grew softer and more fluid. My long, black-stockinged legs caught his attention once, and then again. A faint ring of unspecified longing crept into his voice. His gaze inched up my body, lingering for a while on the gap between the lapels of my black suit jacket—I wore no blouse beneath it. He shifted his shoulders subtly. It was so endearing to watch him try, unobtrusively, to find a more revealing vantage point. Such a tender young adventurer.

That was when I told myself to stop being lax. My flight boarded in less than half an hour and, if I could stay away from him until then, I wouldn't be tempted to do anything stupid. We would both be safe on the plane, surrounded by passengers.

I stood up and shouldered my purse. "Well, I think I will find the ladies' and freshen up before the flight. It was nice to meet you." I smiled down at him with all the benevolence I could manage, quietly bidding farewell to this delicate morsel of youth.

For a moment he looked disappointed and then, without warning, he began babbling. "I like older women, you know? I think they're so sexy. You're very attractive and not so old. But you think I am too young for you, yes?"

Not so old. I had to stifle a laugh. "I *know* you are," I said, smiling.

Quickly I turned and walked down the length of the hall toward the facilities, forcing myself to concentrate on the sound of my heels clicking and echoing percussively off the hard, Soviet surfaces. I inhaled deeply, trying to imagine I could smell Lenin's embalmed body, thirty kilometers away, sleeping in his silent tomb.

In the sterile light of the deserted ladies' room, I saw tiny beads of sweat glistening along the line of my upper lip in the mirror. I could hardly breathe, thinking about how close my escape, and his, had been.

"Good girl, Marta," I said to my reflection in the mirror. I praised myself for my forbearance and self-denial, all the while feeling chilled as the heat of my skin slowly dissipated, like my voice, into the silence of the room. The cold water I splashed liberally on my face and neck forced me to catch my breath. It felt good and real—a blessed distraction from the screaming hunger. Blotting away the droplets with a wad of paper towels, I jumped as I heard the door squeal open, and looked back up into the mirror.

In that split second, a surge of rage overwhelmed me. This idiot boy—this piece of sweetmeat—I had spared him and yet there he was, following me, like a lamb to the slaughter.

"I'm not too young." His voice quavered, sounding almost plaintive.

It must have taken him no small amount of courage to follow me in there, and the adrenaline still tainted his muscles, making him shaky. The smell of it seeped through his skin. I turned slowly, leaving his beautiful image forever static in the mirror.

"You have no idea what you're doing, boy. Go away," I whispered harshly, counting the pulses of blood as they hammered against my eardrums.

One, two, three...

"Turn around and walk out, little dove."

Four, five, six...

"Go now. Go!"

Seven, eight, nine...

Too late and far beyond my control, I was on him in a flash, pushing his back against the cold tile wall. The speed frightened him and now the scent of his youth mingled with the sharp, sweet smell of fear.

Waste not, want not.

That's what I thought as I kissed him, falling onto those plump, angelic lips so eager to be kissed. They parted beneath mine like wet, ripe fruit. I ate and I ate, sucking each of them in turn into my mouth, stroking their length with my tongue. Beneath my hips, he came brilliantly alive, his jean-covered cock a desperate hunter-seeker, blind and straining for a target. If I was going to take what I needed, I could at least give him what he had come looking for first.

I snaked a hand between us—unbuttoning, unzipping and releasing him. Red blossoms of chaotic energy throbbed and died behind my eyelids as I held his cock in my hand. There was so much life there, pushing forward, driving against me mindlessly, helplessly.

He made the most delicious noises, like a baby mammal desperate to find a spare, milked-filled teat. But his hands weren't nearly as innocent. After fumbling with the buttons on my jacket, they grabbed and squeezed feverishly at my breasts, but only long enough to stroke my nipples to erection.

Hot little hands, greedy and impatient, they were off again in search of new territory, traveling downward, along my sides and onto my hips. He pulled them and ground himself savagely against them, trapping my hand between us.

Desire flooded from his pores so thick and pungent that the essence of it almost choked me. I pulled my lips away to see his eyes, half closed. His head tilted back against the wall. He was panting frantically as he grappled for handfuls of my skirt and rucked it up between us.

"God!" he cried out, turning me, pressing me to the wall. "I want to fuck you, now…"

"Of course you do," I murmured soothingly, raising one leg to wrap it around his hips. "Come on, then." My hand, still full of his burning desire, guided his cockhead to my entrance—impatient, hungry, and wet.

He thrust up and in fluidly. The look on his face was heart-breaking as he entered; so much ecstasy in a fraction of a moment held him static. I smiled and watched, knowing that pleasure had blinded him.

"Is this what you wanted?"

He whimpered once and began to fuck slowly and with intensity. His cock felt unbearably sweet, filling me with each plunge, growing thicker as he pushed deeper.

"Oh, god..." he cried again.

His body began to shudder after only a few thrusts. He was so sweet, so gratifyingly enthusiastic; it was impossible not to forgive him for his unseemly lack of endurance. So sad that he would never get the chance to learn to last a little longer. In my arms, the boy's frame shook hard and he drove faster, pumping himself into my heat and toward his final release.

I cupped the back of his neck with my fingers and pulled his head onto my shoulder. His skin was pale and velvet smooth. A sinuous river of life pulsed hypnotically beneath the surface. It spoke to me like the snake in the tree, as it always does. *Taste this and know me,* it hissed.

As he began to orgasm, I bit down into that beautiful valley of flesh at the side of his throat. He jerked as I punctured through to the artery, giving one last thrust and erupting hot and thick inside of me. As I absorbed him into my bloodstream, I could taste the echo of his seed, musky and bitter, just before the coppery flavor of his blood overwashed it.

I almost fainted with pleasure. Sweet youth distilled and vibrant concentrated energy flooded through me in hot, twin fountains. I hardly noticed he was crying out then, his muscles convulsing as he came and came and began to die.

The room was shaded against the early morning light. The air smelled dry and dusty. Daniel was lying stretched out on his wicker divan, fanning himself lazily. He looked at me through the gloom. I hated him like this—in his self-satisfied, grand poobah incarnation. But I also felt acutely defensive and shifted my weight from foot to foot as I gave him a rundown of how the trip had gone.

"So you switched all the bonds?"

"Of course. Rohner agreed that it was a wise move," I said, distracted. There was no escaping it, no avoiding it.

I took a big breath and, with some trepidation, told him what happened at the airport.

"Marta, you know better than that!" Daniel growled, raising himself up in indignation. His anger was palpable. The cat, which had been sleeping by his feet, jumped down and fled in fear.

Katerina and Benedict, who'd been playing draughts and only half listening, both sat up and stared at me. If my confession had rendered any of them speechless at first, they certainly all found their voices eventually. I listened to a barrage of accusations.

"I know, I know…" I said softly, attempting to placate them. "You have every right to be infuriated. I know the rules. They're good rules. I just…I couldn't help myself."

"This sort of shit brings trouble down on all of us, Marta," yelled Daniel, getting to his feet. He stopped about five paces from where I stood and glared at me in disgust. "I thought you looked too damn pink for having spent fourteen hours in transit."

I offered him an apologetic grin and back-stepped a little. Daniel was not particularly violent but he didn't take kindly to any member of his brood breaking the house rules. You don't live for three hundred years and let people trample all over you. I could see he was trying to control his temper. The others in the room snickered.

Drawing his hands over his lean, handsome face and threading them through his silky black hair, Daniel sighed. There were tiny lines at the corners of his eyes and small creases in his cheeks. He hadn't fed in a while. I was sure he would have taken the boy himself had he had the chance. Finally, he settled his hands on his hips.

"Why couldn't you have just waited till Mumbai, Marta? It's not as if you're a newborn. You're not without stamina or self-control. You know what the punishment for a breach like this is."

"I tried to avoid him, Daniel, I swear. I really, really did. But he came begging for it. He followed me, for god's sake! I'm not that strong. No one is. If you could have seen him, you'd be a little more understanding! He was irresistible, Daniel…"

"Tell me you cleaned up properly, Marta. Just tell me that," he said, with a low, measured voice, leveling his gaze at me.

"Well, in a sense, yes."

Daniel's hand flew out and grabbed my throat. "What the fuck does that mean?" He yanked me toward him, his face only inches from mine.

"Well, actually…he's outside in the hall," I wheezed.

"You irresponsible bitch!" The final consonant sprayed my face with his saliva. "You turned him?"

I was shaking and trying to breathe shallowly through my compressed windpipe. None of us actually need to breathe, but it feels terribly uncomfortable not to. "Just…just wait till you meet him before you murder me, okay?"

I could feel his temper; his breath was quick and hot against my face. Then, as if too disgusted to bear the closeness, he pushed me away, hard, and sent me stumbling backward. I fought to keep my balance but my heels wobbled and turned, taking me down.

He stalked away, fuming.

"I'm sorry, Daniel. I really am," I said quietly, struggling back to my feet, dusting my skirt down. I walked to the door. "Just wait till you see him."

Opening the double doors, I poked my head into the hall. "Come in and meet the family."

The boy sauntered in, more graceful now than he had ever been in life. My dead heart fluttered when I thought of how I might have simply drained him and left him on the cold floor of the bathroom at Sheremetyevo. No—he was too precious, too beautiful, and besides, someone needed to teach him how to fuck properly.

I drew him farther into the darkened room. "Stefan? This is Daniel."

The boy smiled shyly before trying to cover it with the bravado of the young. "Hi. Hey, this is so cool!"

Daniel gave the boy a curt nod, but I could see the look of appreciation in his eyes. Katerina got up and came forward, wrapping a lithe arm around the new arrival's shoulders. "Oh, Marta. He's just adorable."

Before I could wipe the smug smile off my face, Daniel looked at me again. "You know the rules, Marta. Down to the hole. Now."

"The hole? Please Daniel, not the hole."

"Yes, the fucking hole. A month."

"A whole month?" I said. The thought of the endless hours of nothingness terrified me. "Couldn't you find it in your heart to go a little easy on me this time? I mean…look at him!"

Daniel's jaw was set hard. He wasn't going to change his mind. Rules were rules. "Thirty days," he said. "I hope he was worth it."

I nod into the hot, damp darkness and shift a little. The bones of my spine bite into my flesh as I lean back against the rough wall of the tiny cell. My skin feels so parched, I imagine I can hear it cracking as I move. In the span of my lifetime, twenty-two days is not so long, and I endure it by remembering the taste of his youth.

WAIT UNTIL DARK, MONTRESOR

Thomas S. Roche

The town of San Esteban is best reached by car on State Route 13, which slips off Interstate 101 with subtlety, implying it doesn't wish to be noticed. Watch for the exit south of Ukiah, make your pukey, carsick way through the Coast Range and be sure to stop for an espresso and a home-baked brownie at Space Cowboy's shack just past the Chatelaine Reservoir about a half-hour past Bargerville. Ask him if you can have one of the "green" brownies; they're made with butter sautéed in Humboldt Honey grown deep and wild in the forest behind SC's place. Eat half and you'll reach San E singing "Uncle John's Band" whether you like the Dead or not.

When she sinks into you she'll appreciate the sweet taste of Honey; she doesn't get out to Space Cowboy's much lately, as they recently had a falling out.

There are a couple of inexpensive options for appropriate lodging in San Esteban. You could hit Sam's Motel down by the boardwalk, but you'll want to be sure not to stay in Room 217.

Otherwise, you'll never get any sleep because of all the hissing whispers of "REDRUM!" from the room's resident ghost, who happens to have croaked at age thirteen, the year he was absolutely fucking obsessed with *The Shining*. You could also go to the Seven Sisters B&B, which is homier and only costs about a ten-spot more than Sam's, but staying there could conceivably find you drugged, bound to a stone altar in the backyard and slit from nuts to noggin so that the Dark Tentacle Goddess of the Ancient Catalonian Death Cults can sup ravenously on your steaming entrails. That, of course, would only happen if you stumbled into the place on one of the High Holy Days, but it's hard to plan for that since those days are rendered on a seven-year cycle in the Proto-Assyrian calendar with esoteric numerology providing the exact days and hours of the required sacrifice. You'd have to go to the Vatican Library just to get a copy of the base-eight figure table and do you want to extract the thirteenth root of a seventy-three-digit number? I know I'd rather not, unless it's absolutely required. Just skip the Seven Sisters unless you get off on living dangerously.

Another option: farther downtown there's the QuikMotel adjacent to the cemetery and next door to the off-leash dog park by the Museum of Antiquities and about a block from the hazardous waste storage yard—no, no, never mind. Forget I mentioned it.

It's probably best to spring for the bill-and-a-half for Lady Jane Grey's just off Maple Street near where the Yuki River meets the Pacific; it's very close to the Beach Blend. After it happens, you'll be weak. You'll want to get to bed fast, and you'll be in no condition to drive.

Check in to your hotel, Montresor; maybe shower, maybe shave if you're that kind of person. You don't have to dress up, but if you're that kind of person, you may want to play to her weaknesses. High black boots are appreciated on both men and women. She favors tight pants over skirts in girls; boys, wear a kilt and she'll love you. If you're up for going the extra mile, she gets weak in the knees over Revlon Blue Black 12 like any good child of the '80s. Do *not* wear perfume, cologne, or body oil; you would not fucking believe how sensitive her sense of smell is. Boys, she likes eyeliner. Girls, just a slut's worth of lipstick will do the trick. Everyone else, it's the earrings—make sure they draw attention to your pretty, pretty throat; long and bright and dangly is always, always good.

Wait until dark, Montresor, before you go to her: the moon must be overhead, because she's our bitch mother, the patron saint of café-bound hungry ghosts. It's not a bad place for a pickup, really, with the moon shining: the Beach Blend has huge windows, so you can see her cocky smile. It's open 24/7, the refuge of cops and criminals, the only place in town to serve decent coffee at 3:00 a.m. She'll show up at sundown so you've got a nice big window of time to work with. She's well known in town as the funky goth girl who's been there for fucking ever, but don't ask around. It makes you conspicuous, and nobody, but nobody wants that in a town like San Esteban.

You'll find her at the back table. Some nights she only writes for three or four hours before retiring upstairs alone for Netflix Giallo movies and Franzia. Other nights she'll sit scribbling madly from twilight-on-the-Yuki until the hot Ukrainian girl behind the counter has to remind her, urgently, that dawn is approaching. Then she'll gather her things and scamper upstairs with a glare at Valechka that could melt iron nails: they always want to kill the messenger.

If she's there she'll be jotting away on some strange sheets of foolscap paper. She's got her cheap burgundy, rudely enough, on an adjacent table, because she can't risk a spill. She always uses fountain pen; it's a habit she never broke. She could be writing in longhand or sketching; she does that sometime, in which case she'll use graphite pencil or black felt architecture pens. There are great gray maps sketched like spiderwebs through black metal filing cabinets upstairs; the writer's fondest fans may never, ever see these, because they contradict each other. She can't stand contradictions.

If she's working furiously, have a seat and enjoy some of the fine Beach Blend—decaf only, Montresor, as you do *not* want to see this girl stressed out. Observe her. Yeah, no shit it's creepy, but you're far from the first.

You've seen her author photos, so you already know this is not what could be called a conventionally beautiful woman. Taken out of the flowing black form-shrouding dress that looks like a burial shroud, her spindly form might be attractive, but her face would never be cast even as an extra for "Buffy" or *Twilight*; it'd fit in better in *The Nightmare Before Christmas*. Her tallness and slimness would still grab attention if she ever went outside; skeegy septuagenarians on Maple Street would still try to talk to her about Marilyn Manson. But since she lives upstairs from the Beach Blend in an old converted attic, she never goes outside—except once a year in September, when she remembers the real Montresor and you do *not* want to be the guy she fucks when she comes back from visiting his grave.

She is possibly nineteen, or appears so, pale, with a straight course of slick blonde hair. Every couple of years she allows Revlon #12 one last chance. She gets green, and wears a turban for a few weeks.

Wait for the smile: wait for the wicked little smile on her wicked little face. When she looks up and breathes deep and has a faint little smile on her face, you'll know she's reasonably happy with the night's output, and she'll be ready to party.

Approach her respectfully.

"I'm sorry to interrupt you, but are you Jen Jacobs?"

She'll look shy, nervous; make her soft bright ripe eyes roll, but she's handing you a load of bullshit. She'll be glowing with pride. Christ, this bitch loves being famous. She'll giggle; actually, it's more like a tweet.

"Yes, I am. Do I know you?"

You won't recognize the voice from the podcasts. She really has to concentrate to get that smoky seductive sound to it, and with her intermittently acute social anxiety it just never happens in public.

"No," you'll tell her, "but I'm a huge fan. I've read every one of your books."

Gush a little, if you'll forgive the rather vivid pun. Girls, it helps if you flutter a little bit, maybe look like you're going to faint. If you're that kind of guy, go that route as well. If you're of the manly sort, maybe act all shy and aw-shucks and tell her how amazed you are to meet her and you love how she captures the essence of the character's soul. Give her reason to think you're not fucking with her; cite chapter and verse where her books made you cry, or how some catch in her voice during a podcast or audiobook really chilled you to your soul, Montresor; snow her.

She's Jen fucking Jacobs: obviously, she gets gushed at all the time. But listen to me very carefully, Montresor: it never, ever gets old.

She'll blush, an easy feat when you're pale as fresh milk. She'll start clearing the pages and invite you to sit down.

"I couldn't. I couldn't possibly. Really? Oh my god, I'm having coffee with Jen Jacobs. If you don't mind my saying so, I just can't believe that you're so young!"

"Oh, I'm really not," she'll say. "It's just in my genes. Do I really look that young?" You'd think she'd be used to it by now. She'll tee-hee, a sound like the too-sweet wine she favors. That's not her sexy podcast laugh, and it's not her real laugh; if she's nervous (which she is), her real guffaw is a sound not unlike a donkey pissed off about hauling watermelons.

Oh, you'll hear the podcast laugh. The one vampires always make just before they rip your throat out. I think you're going to like it: it's smooth, wet, cruel, sad, seductive, so very unlike sweet wine, and so much like hard liquor. You'll remember it forever after, like you remember the soft subtle whisper of your very first "I love you," Montresor: sadly, with pain, fear, misery, regret and longing.

Reassure Jen Jacobs that, in fact, she looks young. She'll blush and say, "Genes, gwah-haww!!" and nervously Bogart her coffee cup.

This age thing is a growing problem, according to her agent; she shouldn't even be in public. She's got maybe five more years before people start to freak; she's looked nineteen for a decade and a half now, since the publication of her first book, in which her bio said she was sixteen.

She'll try to buy you a coffee. Buy her one instead, and you'll have to insist: "It's the least I can do for all the pleasure your writing has brought me." Some bullshit like that. She'll probably make that weird mule sound: no, really, it's laughter.

I cannot emphasize this enough: Jen Jacobs craves the adulation of her fans even more than she wants the more juicy thing you have to offer. But she distrusts her fans as she distrusts herself; she'll want to know you've really read her books. If you haven't, you can spend $1.19 on Amazon and pick up a copy of überfan Vladimira Chernobyl's *The Darkspeaker Bible,* the closest thing you'll find to Cliff's Notes for ultraviolent erotic vampire romance snuff. Ask her real questions you really want to know the answers to; she's heard them all, but writers never get tired of hearing themselves talk.

You will notice a few things about Jen Jacobs as she nervously holds court self-indulgently. If you ask her abstract questions about history or society, you will find her slipping occasionally: "Back in the '60s," "In the old days," "Baudelaire," "Rabelais," "Winston Churchill," "The Terror," "The Crisis," "The Troubles," and then she'll blush and stammer and try to cover up by making like a history geek and lamely mentioning some book she read on the subject.

She has read books on the subject—every subject, but that's not why she mentions the Boer War with sadness and a tremble to her voice. And please don't say the name Byron.

There are a couple of other things not to ask her. First, don't inquire about the name, which is of course a pseudonym, and a strange one for someone who writes epic group sex vampire snuff porno laced with the sharp hiss of matchlocks and scented with the ripe metallic tang of bursting smallpox boils. This name is the remnant of her early writing career, when she tried to be good—and then failed. She kept the name and lost the pretensions, but she's still a bit sensitive about it; her first choice was Reynard-Pierre Seine-Saint-Denis, so you and her agent should count your lucky stars.

And second, don't ask her about Montresor, Montresor—the *real* Montresor. You're just a stand-in, the cheapest date a vamp could ever hope for. This question is the reason she no longer appears on midnight panels at the San Diego Comic-Con, no longer hosts the annual all-night vampire slam at San Francisco's ConSanguinUity. Don't ask her why she called the second-person protagonist "Montresor" in her best-selling vampire trilogy *Darkspeaker.* If you must know, Montresor was a saucy nickname she used for a very special guy because his savage sadistic countenance and fondness for rattling chains reminded her of the perp in that most straightforward of all Poe's snuff stories, and the *Darkspeaker* trilogy, all five volumes, 4,320 pages and 1,512,000 words of it, was her way of sobbing through the loss of him. Bringing him up might even make her cry.

Montresor, Montresor is the reason you're never going to get a second date; he's the reason you'll stumble, soon, blood-drained and happy, *away*, never to return, because a ghost watches over her, jealous and cruel just like every ghost is, and the man who returns, or woman, is the woman, or man, who dies. She knows this, I believe, somewhere inside, and the fear is what drives her, even more than the sadness. That she's trapped is self-evident. That it's love, after ten minutes, ten decades or ten thousand years, is what I'm telling you now: show the girl a good time, Montresor, and then move on. It's bad taste to linger, Montresor, and far worse for your health than a vampire's bite could ever, ever be. Think in moments.

When the time feels right, steer the convo toward matters intimate; for all her predatory nature Jen Jacobs is not unlike a frightened cat. She's not quite sure if she can trust you to rub her belly without having her claws ready to dig. You may need to point the camera on you, briefly, just to convince her you're there for her; mention a recent breakup, establishing you're single; you're not sure you're down for anything serious. But gosh, you know, sometimes it's just so good to be intimate with someone, no strings attached.

Jen will like that—no strings attached.

You might want to mention you'll be back on the road tomorrow. Say how nobody knows you've dropped by this town, you weren't expecting it, the place is so charming. That doesn't really matter, since she's not that kind of girl. But once upon a time it was so very important that no one would know where you went or just who might have eaten you. Say it, and she's putty, Montresor. Putty that sucks you.

There'll be an awkward lapse in conversation. You'll have been talking, then, for an hour, maybe two. She'll look a bit pink because it's dirty, what she's thinking, because she barely knows you. She's done it a thousand times in this café alone, but at heart she's a good girl, and now you're her Tim Curry.

Break the lapse in conversation by asking one of two things.

If Jen's still seeming nervous, say "Do you really live upstairs from here?"—which she's mentioned in her podcast a dozen times, that she lives in a loft upstairs from a certain café in Santa Carla, which is her fictional stand-in for San Esteban. Anyone who's really listened to her podcast, or read her blog, would know such a thing and guess that this is the café. San Esteban is the bitch's Cannery Row, and you're just an extra, passing through.

If she's gone kind of languid, though, a soft slow bob to the movements of her head and maybe a red tongue licking red lips, her eyes on your eyeliner, a flirty little cock to her head and maybe a stretch, stretch, stretch, her back arched and her nipples showing through the thin cotton fabric of the dress that seemed loose just a moment ago—then don't bother asking where she lives. Just say, "Would you like to go somewhere private?"

Jen will smile, touch your hand. She's a slut, a torrid, horrid slut for doing such a thing right here in public where her fans could see, just an hour or an hour and a half after she's met you. But she kinda gets off on that, which is how this whole stupid vampire thing got started so many long sad lonely years ago.

She'll lead you upstairs; she'll leave her things at the counter and tell the stacked blonde Ukrainian barista, "I'll be back for these later," receiving from Valechka an icy stare while the coffee girl unconsciously fingers her own throat. Jen will then come-hither/frogwalk you back past the roaster and up past the grinder to the four flights of stairs. She may kiss you halfway up, maybe even put her hands places, or encourage you to do such a thing. Her teeth may show when she chews on you; sometimes she can't help herself.

Look, if that happens, don't you freak out at this point. Never be a prick tease, Montresor: it's bad, very bad, for your health.

Her loft is on the top floor—a beautiful, big, open, airy, moonlit jumbled mess, with the velvet blackout curtains pulled back so the floor-to-ceiling windows show either night sky or fog, probably fog. Depending on what time you showed up and what time of year it is, it could be anywhere from 8:00 p.m. to midnight; June to November the moon may describe a glorious arc from one end of this great bank of windows to the other. You could cry from that view, but she's heard the compliments a thousand times, and she's got two things on her mind: blood and sex, the double-barreled shotgun of interpersonal relations.

She'll be all over you, kissing, caressing, undressing. Her hands move fast—inhumanly fast. You'll be stripped naked and shivering by the time she hurls you heavy, hard and panting across the bed, because they like the flesh goose bumped and it's been a long time since fear alone did it for her. She'll be on top of you, fully dressed; if you try to undo her, she'll slap your hands away. She'll get your wrists pinned down over your head, and she'll look down at you, probably, and breathe hard and draw back and show fang. If you struggle...well, don't.

And here it happens: she *asks*. Believe it? A thousand times Montresor told her: never ask, s/he might say no.

"You don't mind, do you?" she'll say, and it's a new voice, an old voice: the Jen Jacobs of the podcasts-lectures-audiobooks: it's the voice of San E's sexy predator, come home to Feed. If anyone gets to this point and is surprised he's about to be eaten...well, don't.

She might have asked beforehand, but frankly, until those fangs are out, all the way out, the poor girl is just too freakin' shy. If a stiff prick has no conscience…just show her, Montresor, show her your throat.

If you don't answer, she'll look guilty, she'll look shy, her milk-pale face will blush hot pink and she'll say it again, with a hint of her old self, a hint of *Have I done something wrong, sir/ma'am?*

She'll ask you, voice small: "Do you mind?"

You'll say no. Or you won't; I don't give a fuck, Montresor. You've read the books, or at least their Amazon summaries—and probably stroked to them. You've heard her best podcasts, and if you somehow got in over your head then you've always wanted to go there.

You'll say no, and Jen will lean down and purr a little, and you'll smell her sweet wine-breath; she'll slide off of you and glance up toward the moonlight to make sure you can see her, because she needs that. If you can't, because of fog or clouds or lack of moon, then she'll light a few candles, maybe turn on a black light, like any child of the '80s. Then her slim white hands will work magic on buttons, and her burial shroud will go shimmying down her white body leaving her pale, nude, and glowing in the moonlight.

Her breaths will come slow as she circuits the bed; her bright breasts will heave, nipples standing pink and firm from them. She will course slowly around you like a shark at the inception of its frenzy. You will tremble at the bestial little growls. You will goose bump toes-to-toupee from the keening sound that comes out of her mouth.

You know it so well: it's the sound vampires make when they're hot for it. Mother*fuck*er: it's real.

She's on you so fast you don't even see her move; nobody ever does, which is beautiful. Time-lapse photography of this moment would be gorgeous, but only three Russians ever managed to try that—and they're not on Facebook.

Will she toy with you? Probably not. If she does, fucker, *mazel tov*. If not, just surrender: there's pleasure in death, sweet Montresor, or we wouldn't be having this conversation.

The initial penetration is far more painful than anything you've ever experienced. Suffice it to say that Jen has acoustic foam behind every possible surface throughout her top-story loft; those windows, for all their hugeness, are double-paned. You will scream, and not stop until you're just plain too weak to continue. When you're at that point, you'll still be screaming, or think you are, but no sound will come out: just a light sweet keening sound, like a prayer, only filthy.

This is it—the moment you understand that I was not fucking around; I was not making this up. The ugliest, prettiest parts of the *Darkspeaker* trilogy were not fiction or fantasy. They were memoir, friend: not verbatim, but close.

Her mouth will work on you; your naked body will arch against her. Her sharp painted claws will dig into you—chest, tits, belly, arms, ass, it doesn't matter—and the pain will distract you while she gets her other hand up in your hair, if you have some, and holds you in place so she can drink still more deeply, and that's when your soul makes a slurping sound, pouring into Jen's body. If you didn't think you had one...um, sorry, Montresor, you did and you don't. God, I fucking love this part.

Your soul is hot and wet and soothing and terrifying, and Jen's a messy eater. Between wet awful slurping sounds at your carotid artery—or maybe at your jugular if she's feeling naughty that night—you'll feel the faint soft splatters. You'll taste salt, you'll taste iron. You think if she Feeds you then you really won't die, but come on—were you counting on that? I seriously fucking hope not; what is this, a stroke story?

It is only your blood that you taste: that is one thing about which Jen Jacobs is exceedingly meticulous. Not a touch of her essence will get anywhere near to you, because that causes complications, and the poor sad girl really hates that.

If you were the real Montresor, back from the dead and still watching, sure—but that ship sailed long, long ago.

When you're empty she'll give you a moment, to feel what life's like without a soul. Interesting, huh? A million things could go through your head, but to be honest you're too busy panicking.

Then she'll feed yourself back to you, in a hot kiss with the sweet sick sad whisper of sin, Montresor. How it hurts, Montresor, how it fucking hurts having a soul. Bad form to start crying at this point, but don't worry; it happens.

She may fuck you, then; in fact, she probably will, since you'll be hard and she'll be wet, or you'll be wet and she'll be wet, or maybe she'll be hard too if she's packing that night—it's been known to happen. And you're too weak to struggle so she's got two free hands. While she feeds you, she fucks you—naked on top of you, sometimes weeping herself, because it hurts as much to give it up as it does to take it back.

Montresor is the reason you'll walk out of here, friend. He is why Jen gives you back your soul, because she tried the thing once, Montresor, killing and resurrecting, as the others do—and that, sad to say, ended in tears. Don't tempt her. It's bad for your health.

This, too, will end in tears, if it didn't begin that way: Yours, uncontrollable. How butch, bad, manly, studly, stony are you? Be her whiny little bitch for ten minutes. If you've never cried during sex before, there's a first time for everything.

She'll curl up and hold you and stroke your brow and caress

your face and whisper, "There, there, baby, there, there." Her voice will be podcast quality, and it will warm you inside as she comforts you. She'll pat your head soothingly with a hand that's done awful things not a few moments before. Her fingernails will be bloody and pregnant with strips of your skin.

But you'll take it, and surrender it, and you might even say, "Thank you," and you'll almost certainly say, "I love you." She will not say it back. If you're a genuine fan, you'll be thinking *I've made it with Jen Jacobs,* and if you're one of those types you'll already be writing the blog post, the Tweet, the true confession to email your fanfic friends.

No one will ever believe you, you know; it's just another brand of slash, the "I Fucked the Author" flavor, wicked and disconcerting but really, Montresor, not very original.

Relish those creative thoughts, Montresor, because they'll help you transition. They'll help you forget that not minutes before, your immortal soul rested in the drooling mouth of a predator, who spared you because of some sad sick fucker you'll never meet. Compose your new blog post and cry.

She'll let you sleep. If she thinks you're out, she might talk to you, then, or talk *at* you; she might issue a few true confessions, apologies, recriminations, regrets. If it's one of those rare nights when her heart feels the burden, and she wants to unload, she might say more. She might even tell you the story of the real Montresor, and as long as you haven't had any caffeine before meeting her, then that would be a truly beautiful thing. If you're sleeping, well…don't. Words are precious. Stay awake for them.

Any story she tells you will be sad, like the *Darkspeaker* trilogy, only a thousand times more improbable because Jen Jacobs is a child of the '80s, and back then we believed things, beautiful things, agonizingly beautiful things that seem fucked-up in retrospect, but can still make you cry. We believed in the possibilities of the future and the power of love—go ahead and laugh. Jen was a dreamer, a romantic, pitted selflessly against the Victorians and Imperialists with their cold cruel plans for world domination and sexual repression: diamonds in the Congo, Montresor, and a million shriveled hands. We believed, then; we believed in hearts, and after a century of mourning hers still beats, pumping ice water but wanting something more, which is more than I can say for most of us. That is why you'll live.

At some point, she'll rise off of you; she'll wipe herself down, wipe you down; she'll unshackle you. As long as you haven't been a horrible cad or a wretched bitch, she'll invite you to shower with her. You'll be weak, but she's got a grab rail, and she'll support you with her preternatural strength. Don't worry; she won't let you fall. She's not that type of vampire.

When you're no longer goose bumped and you're able to stand despite being a quart low, it's time to say bye-bye. Don't ask for her number. Don't imply you'll be back. Down that path lies madness, and madness is ugly.

She shows you to the door. No kiss good-bye, Montresor; you'll regret it.

It's a short walk to Lady Jane Grey's, where you've got your computer. You should resist the urge to write it all down right away. Just put up the DO NOT DISTURB sign, take off your clothes and crash into starched white sheets and dream it all again, and you can write up the blog post later. Nobody's going to believe you, anyway. Jen Jacobs, author of the *Darkspeaker* trilogy, writer of filthy ultradecadent vampire fiction that's corrupted the souls of young people nationwide—a vampire? Clever, Montresor, very clever. It sounds like you almost believe it yourself.

Sleep until dark, Montresor. For at least a few days the direct sun is going to do funny things to you, and your night vision will be better than your day. Don't eat before leaving; you're still digesting your own soul, and if there's one thing you don't need it's to get that shit mixed up with a double cheeseburger and fries.

I also strongly suggest you don't drive down Main Street and take a sick slow circuit past the Beach Blend Café, leaning over, peering in. I implore you to skip it, but you won't.

She might be there, scribbling furiously, or maybe putting the moves on some new hot young thing—guy, girl, conspicuously genderfucky other; we go with the flow in San Esteban, and Jen Jacobs is nothing if not open-minded.

Or she might not be there; she could have slept in, or be upstairs crying, which she does sometimes, when she thinks about him, usually the day after a really good feeding. It might be weeks before another blog post, another podcast; in that case, Montresor, you should feel in some way gratified. But do not under any circumstances go inside.

You might feel it, then, the ghost of a lover watching you, someone who knows what you've been through. You might feel his breath on the back of your neck, or his fingers on your shoulder. You might even hear a voice whispering: "Thanks, dude. She needed that."

Look, now…I mean well. I'm trying to be nice, but all it'll do is scare the bejeezus out of you. So let's not, and say we did: just know I appreciate it, 'cause she's lonely. She's so very, very lonely.

You can get on 13 at the far end of Main Street; it's a slow forty-five over the hills to 101, and Space Cowboy's will almost certainly be closed. If the moon's overhead, Montresor, say a prayer to her, for all the things she's given you and all the sad sick beautiful things she's taken away, or never, thankfully, let you taste with your tragedies.

And then flip the moon off, if you're that sort of person; it never hurts to keep the bitch guessing.

In pace requiescat!

THE TEMPTATION OF MLLE. MARIELLE DOUCETTE

Anna Black

Marielle Doucette, once the *poule de luxe* of a Marquis and, recently, a prisoner at the *Conciergerie*, sighed as she bathed in the tub of hot water. The last time she had had a bath was the night before she was arrested—a pail of cold water and a coarse cloth. As for her arrest, the envious bitch who owned the pastry shop where she worked had accused Marielle of being a counterrevolutionary.

Marielle angrily scrubbed her arms. Counterrevolutionary! She couldn't have cared less about the Revolution. Men were men. Wearing the *tricoleurs* did not make them any better. If anything, it had made most of them worse.

Liberté, égalité, fraternité, ou la mort!

That had been the battle cry of the people when they rose up against the aristocrats but now there was more death in the streets than liberty or equality.

The shop owner accused her of being a counterrevolutionary because she'd grown tired of her husband lusting after Marielle.

But who could blame him; his wife had been as flat as a boy, and her head would have looked quite at home on the neck of a mule.

None of it mattered to the Revolutionary Tribunal; not the petty charge or Marielle's pleas for mercy. They had found her guilty, for they knew she'd once been the mistress of a Marquis and to be the former whore of an aristocrat was as bad as being an aristocrat.

Marielle frowned as she looked down at the dirty water. She was no more an aristocrat than those who had condemned her to the guillotine. She rose from the tub. Just as she reached for a towel, the door opened and a man walked in.

His name was Armand. He was the one who, somehow, had secured her freedom from prison and brought her to this chateau near the Palais Royal. At first, she had been so happy to be free she had not questioned why he had freed her. Now she wondered what he wanted with her.

He stopped in front of her. His dark eyes raked her naked body. She did not blush nor try to cover herself. Such modesty had been ripped from her years ago.

"Put on your robe," he said.

Marielle stared at him. Although he was clearly a peasant, with his wide shoulders and muscular body, he was also quite attractive, and it was clear from the intense look he gave her that he found her equally desirable.

"Why should I?"

"Go naked then. My master wants to see you now that you no longer stink of the prison."

"Your master? Who is he?"

He only looked at her, his gaze so lustful that Marielle's body responded. Her nipples tightened and the cleft between her legs tingled. She stepped out of the tub, picked up the towel, and dried herself. Armand watched as she rubbed the cloth over her high, firm breasts and between her slim thighs. The cloth gently chafed the soft lips of her sex.

She sighed.

At the sound, Armand's nostrils flared, like a stallion sensing a mare in heat, but he remained still and silent.

Once she was done, she put on the robe. "You may now take me to this master of yours."

Armand led her out of the room and down the corridor until they arrived at a huge door. He opened it and gestured for her to enter. Sheets covered most of the furniture in the room but a few chairs and couches were uncovered. And on one of those chairs sat a man.

Marielle could not make him out. He sat in the shadows, and the only light came from a few candles scattered about the room.

Armand nudged her hard in the back. Marielle flashed him a quick glare but moved closer, and then gasped, "You!"

The man, who was dark, lean, and handsome, laughed. "I gather you're not happy to see me, mademoiselle."

Marielle balled her hands into fists, as much from fear as anger. "Why should I be?"

He smiled, his fangs flashing between his firm lips. "Because I am your rescuer."

"You're nothing but a monster, Chrétien Girardin."

"Come, now. Is that any way to speak of your deliverer?"

Marielle turned to Armand. "Take me back to the prison."

Chrétien laughed again and, as he did, the hairs on the back of Marielle's neck stiffened. "You'd rather go back to that hellhole than be with me? You wound my heart, *ma petite*."

Marielle whirled around. "That is impossible, *monsieur*, for we both know you have no heart. Or at least not one that beats.

As for my dying, given that if I stay here I will die anyway, I'd rather die in possession of my immortal soul. Take me back, Armand."

"Armand is my creature, Mademoiselle Doucette. He obeys only me."

"Then command him to return me to the *Conciergerie*. For if I had known you were the instrument of my deliverance, I would have remained there."

Chrétien rose from the chair and grabbed her. He gripped her arms so tightly that she winced but willed herself not to cry out.

"Even now you cling to your pride. You, who were only hours away from the guillotine kissing that pretty neck of yours." He tilted his head and stared at her throat. "When I could find such better uses for it."

Marielle struggled but she might as well have tried to escape from steel chains. "What do you want?"

"Don't play the fool. You know what I want, what I've always wanted." He pulled her hard against him. "You, my beautiful Marielle. Your soft body, your sweet face, and that lust for revenge that I sense within you. Give those to me and you will be spared the death that awaits you if you return to the *Conciergerie*."

"No! I won't become a monster!"

"Then know this. I will not bequeath what you will not take from me freely. However, after wanting you for so long, now that I finally have you, you will be mine. One way or the other." He looked over at Armand. "Take her back to her room."

Armand grabbed her arm and dragged her out of the salon. Marielle struggled to free herself but it was no use. Armand, like Chrétien, was too strong for her. He took her to the room where she had bathed and pushed her inside. Marielle fell to the floor. She heard a key turn in the lock, and leaping up, she beat against the door but all she heard were receding footsteps.

She leaned against the door and wearily closed her eyes. She had thought being in prison was the worst thing that could happen to her. Hadn't she learned by now, especially after all the things that had happened to her since that terrible night five years ago with the Viscount?

There were always worse things—such as being the prisoner of a vampire who wanted to make you a vampire, as well.

Having exhausted herself pounding on the door, Marielle fell asleep. When she awoke, she discovered the door unlocked and quickly put on her clothes. She had no idea where Armand or Chrétien was and she wasn't going to waste time finding out. She silently made her way down the stairs.

Chrétien.

Some said he was a protégé of the Marquis de Sade, others that he was a *gens de couleur* from the French colony of Saint-Domingue who was passing as white. Still others insisted he was a defrocked priest who practiced black masses.

But none of them knew the truth—that Chrétien was a vampire, a secret he had revealed to Marielle when he first tempted her to become his companion of the night. Therefore, she had to go while she had the chance. For she feared she could not long resist him.

Heading toward the front door, she heard the murmur of voices coming from a room to her left. Instinct told her to run but curiosity subjugated instinct. She crept toward the room and looked inside. A fire blazed in the fireplace. Three men were within; Chrétien and Armand, who stood behind the third man. He looked like an aristocrat, but his once-elegant clothes were dirty and torn.

"Please, *monsieur*. If it's money you want, I can get it."

Chrétien loomed over the man. "Even if you had money, my dear Comte, I would not want it."

"But there must be something you want."

"You have nothing I want. Except..."

"Except what, *monsieur*? I still have friends. They will come to the aid of the Comte de Artois."

"Really?" Chrétien smiled coldly. "And would these friends of yours be willing to give me your life?"

The Comte's eyes widened. "No, please, I don't want to die. Your man rescued me from prison. I thought it was because you wanted something from me."

"I do. Your life."

The Comte began sobbing. He reached for Chrétien, but Armand grabbed him and held him firmly. The Comte was now making such a pitiful noise that Marielle found herself feeling sorry for him.

"*Monsieur*, please. Why do you wish to kill me? I have done nothing wrong."

Chrétien smiled, but his smile was like the glittering edge of a knife. "You believe that? That you are innocent?"

"I swear to you that I am. I have harmed no one."

Chrétien made a gesture. Armand twisted the Comte's arm. He screamed and his cry pierced Marielle to her soul.

"Oh, God! Save me! Save me!"

"Tsk, tsk, *monsieur*. My servant hardly hurt you. What noises will you make when he truly goes to work on you?"

"I have a sister," the Comte cried. "She is in hiding but I know where she is. She is a virgin. I give her to you. If you'll only let me live."

Disgust soured Marielle's stomach, and then she realized she had seen the Comte before. He had been a customer of a friend of Marielle's, a girl named Sophie. The Comte had Sophie whipped for having laughed at the size of his penis. She had lingered for a week until God took pity on her and ceased her suffering.

Tears stung Marielle's eyes. Sophie had been a sweet girl who had laughed all the time.

"You will give me your sister," Chrétien mused. "And I can do with her whatever I please?"

"Yes, monsieur. You can fuck her mouth. Or her ass if you like. Or you can have your man fuck her ass while you watch."

"And her blood?"

The Comte's mouth opened like a fish. "What?"

"May I have her blood too?"

"Yes, yes. Whatever you want."

"Tempting." Chrétien shrugged. "But impossible. Your sister is out of my reach."

"What do you mean?"

"Her name is Jeannette?"

The Comte frowned. "Yes."

"She left France weeks ago, with my help, and with her virtue intact. But you have given me an idea. Armand, if you please?"

With one brawny hand holding both the Comte's wrists, Armand used the other to pull down his pants.

"No!" the Comte screamed.

"I will release you," Chrétien said, "but only after Armand fucks you in your ass—while I watch, of course."

"No, please," the Comte blubbered. "I beg you."

"You will allow it or I will kill you right now."

"Oh, God, please, I don't want to die!"

Chrétien nodded to Armand, who opened the front of his pants. Marielle gasped when she saw his cock. It was thick, long, and densely veined. He guided it toward the Comte's buttocks. The man struggled, and then moaned, as Armand nudged the head of his huge cock into monsieur le Comte's ass, and when

Armand began fucking him hard and deep, he screamed.

Marielle's throat tightened. She had seen men pleasuring each other before. There wasn't much in life she had not witnessed since that night her father had given her to the Viscount and his friends but this was different; different in a way that both horrified and mesmerized her.

Perhaps, she thought, it had to do with the fact that the Comte had had Sophie killed and Marielle could not help but feel pleasure in watching him suffer as her friend had.

"Please, monsieur," the Comte pleaded. "Please, stop."

Armand grunted with each thrust of his cock into the Comte's ass. Chrétien only stood, watching coolly, his handsome face betraying nothing. But Marielle noted the flaring of his nostrils.

Suddenly, he reached over and grabbed the Comte's cock, quickly moving his hand back and forth. The Comte threw his head back against Armand's broad shoulder, exposing his long pale neck. He groaned, his mouth working, his eyes closed.

Chrétien moved nearer, his gaze locked on the Comte's throat.

Armand jerked his hips faster, his cock thrusting deep into the Comte's ass while Chrétien stroked the Comte's cock.

The Comte moaned, his body shuddering, and Marielle knew he was climaxing. Armand grunted and he too trembled as his own release gripped him. That was when Chrétien struck. He clamped his mouth onto the Comte's throat. The Comte screamed as Chrétien's fangs sank into his flesh.

Armand stepped away, his cock wet and reddened. He adjusted his clothing. Then he stood and watched as Chrétien drank the Comte's blood. Soon, the only sounds were Armand's labored breathing and the soft, sucking noise of Chrétien feeding.

Marielle gripped the side of the door around which she peered. She should have been horrified watching the vampire drink the Comte's blood but she felt, instead, a creamy sense of satisfaction.

The Comte got what he deserved, not only because of what he'd done to poor Sophie, but for his eagerness to trade his own sister for his pitiful life. He was no better than Marielle's father who had given her to the Viscount to pay off his gambling debts.

Chrétien lifted his head from the Comte's throat. His face was transfixed as if he were in the grip of a powerful orgasm. Blood trickled down the sides of his mouth. He released the Comte's lifeless body and it crumpled to the floor.

Armand handed Chrétien a handkerchief, which he used to clean the blood from around his mouth.

"*Merci.*" Waving the handkerchief, he gestured at the Comte's body. "Get rid of that."

Armand nodded. Chrétien moved past him and headed toward the door.

Marielle ran until she found a place to hide. She watched as the vampire left the ballroom and headed for the stairs, his tall, dark figure moving as swiftly as the night wind.

Freedom was just a few steps away…and also terror and fear and death. She knew, in her heart, that she would not survive out in the world.

She stepped out of her hiding place. "Chrétien!"

He stopped and stared at her for a long moment, and then hurried down the stairs. He picked her up and carried her swiftly back upstairs.

"You can leave, Marielle," he said. "No one will stop you. What I want from you, you must give willingly."

"You killed that man."

Chrétien stared down at her. "Yes."

"I'm glad you killed him."

"Why?"

"He deserved it."

"Do you truly believe that?"

Marielle thought about Sophie. How her laughter had been like the tinkling of silver bells and how, when she finally died, even then, she had laughed at something only she could see.

"Yes," she replied. "I believe it."

Chrétien lifted his head. "Listen."

At first, Marielle heard nothing, and then, in the distance, shots and screams. She shivered.

Chrétien touched her cheek, drawing her attention back to him. "The mob has found another victim. Do not fear. They will not harm you here."

He leaned over and kissed her hair, her cheeks and then, finally, her lips. She opened her mouth and he slid his tongue inside. She tasted blood. The Comte de Artois's blood.

Chrétien drew away and gazed silently down at her.

"I'll become one of the damned," she said, "if I give myself to you."

He shrugged. "Damnation. Salvation. They are no longer any concerns of mine. Nor will they be of yours."

"But you were human once."

"No longer."

"What about your soul?"

"I do not believe I ever had such a thing, not even when I was human."

"I believe I have one."

He smiled indulgently. "Of course, *ma petite*."

"I don't want to go to hell, Chrétien."

"Think, Marielle, of all that you have endured since your father gave you to the Viscount. Was that not hell?"

Marielle lowered her head. He would know about that,

wouldn't he? He gently lifted her chin and she looked up into his dark, infinite eyes.

"If I leave here, I will die, won't I?"

He nodded. "You may remain free for a time. Perhaps you will find someone who could help you escape, but I doubt it. You have no friends, no protectors, and any man you gave yourself to in exchange for passage from France would either give you to another or kill you when he was finished."

A chill spread through Marielle. "You are very blunt."

"I see myself as a rationalist in a time of unreason."

"It can't go on forever—the terror."

Chrétien's upper lip curled. "Can't it?"

She shivered again. He was right. The blood that ran in the streets, the madness that gripped the people; it could go on for years. She needed to be strong enough to survive that. Chrétien could give her that: the strength, the power, the life everlasting.

"I am afraid to die."

"I know, *ma petite*. But you will die only for a moment." He stroked her cheek. "And then I will bring you back and you and I will be together. Forever."

"And I can do to others what you did to the Comte?"

"Yes." One of his eyebrows quirked up. "Do you have someone in mind?"

"I have many in mind, monsieur, but the first is the Viscount who..." She stopped and swallowed thickly. "He has escaped France. The last I heard he was in England."

"Then we will find him, and he will be yours, *ma petite*."

He kissed her again but this time she eagerly licked and sucked at the blood she tasted on his mouth, and then quickly pulled away from Chrétien. "You arranged that, didn't you? What happened with the Comte downstairs? You staged that, because you knew about Sophie."

He smiled. "And was it not sweet to see him pay for what he had done?"

Marielle slowly nodded. "It was. Very sweet."

"Excellent. Now, take off those rags. You will never wear such rubbish again."

Marielle stood before Chrétien, naked, but no longer afraid. Disrobing, he invited her to the bed.

Marielle crawled onto the bed and lay back as Chrétien joined her. He took her in his arms and kissed her, gently, sweetly. And then she heard Armand walk into the room.

"Join us, Armand," Chrétien said.

The old fear rose in Marielle as she watched Armand take off his clothes, revealing his muscular body.

Five men, the Viscount and his friends, staring eagerly at her bound and naked body on the bed.

Chrétien must have felt her trembling. "No, *ma petite*, it will not be like that. I need Armand to give you pleasure so that it will not be so painful when I turn you—and, you will be hungry afterward."

"I don't want to kill him."

"You won't," Chrétien replied.

Armand smiled as he lay on the bed next to Marielle. "Do not fear, mademoiselle."

Chrétien nestled his long body behind her, his groin cupping her buttocks. He caressed her breasts, his long fingers pulling and tugging at her nipples until they were as hard as beads. He moved his hands away, and Marielle watched, trembling, as Armand slowly caressed her naked breasts with his warm lips and moist tongue. Her blood was on fire and her sex throbbed as Armand slowly licked her nipples, and then drew a breast deep into his mouth, sucking it hungrily.

"Bite it," she whispered.

Armand closed his teeth around her nipple.

"Harder."

Chrétien's warm breath caressed her neck.

"Do it," he commanded Armand.

Armand bit her nipple. Marielle hissed as pain and pleasure exploded within her. He gently chewed the tender, heated flesh. As for Chrétien, he firmly took hold of her hips and eased his cock inside her and began fucking her from behind; smooth thrusts that pushed her breast deeper into Armand's mouth.

"*Oh, mon dieu,*" she cried.

Armand released her breast and slowly moved down her body. As Chrétien continued to fuck her, Armand reached her mound and delicately traced his tongue over the lips of her sex, which were spread open by Chrétien's thick cock hammering inside her. Armand feverishly licked her sex, his tongue dancing over her stiffened clit.

Marielle climaxed and, as she did, she felt Chrétien's mouth on her throat, his fangs sinking deep into her flesh. She cried out and Armand buried his face deep inside her sex. He licked her harder and she sensed he was also licking Chrétien's cock where it was speared deep within her.

The world darkened for Marielle as Chrétien drank, his mouth sucking lustily, his low, throaty moans thrumming against her back.

Marielle came again, and her orgasm, now coupled with the sweet pain of Chrétien's feeding, was so intense she stopped breathing.

Armand continued to lick Marielle's sex, his thick tongue rasping over her straining clit, his big, calloused hands squeezing her breasts and pinching her nipples. And as Chrétien fucked her and fed from her, her blood flowing thickly into his mouth, Marielle sensed death, like a shadow on the edge of her sight.

When she climaxed again, screaming out her pleasure, her body twisting between Armand's mouth and Chrétien's cock and fangs, the shadow became night.

Marielle threw back her head, the warm, wet blood flowing down her throat. She straddled the naked body of the Viscount, her hands pressed against the graying hairs on his chest. It was the very same Viscount who, when her father had given her to him as payment for a gambling debt, had raped her, and then allowed his aristocratic friends to do the same.

No pulse beat beneath her palms. She looked at the bloody wound on his throat and smiled.

The door to the Viscount's bedchamber opened. Chrétien moved next to her and gently slid his hand through her hair.

"Well done, *ma petite*."

Marielle crawled off the Viscount's body and into Chrétien's arms. She kissed him deeply. He licked and sucked what remained of the Viscount's blood from her mouth, and she felt his cock thicken between them.

She wanted to fuck him, as she always did after a kill, but she wished to go back to their lodgings here in London where Armand waited for them so that she could have them both.

"I'm finished here," she said.

Chrétien nodded. Marielle put on her gown and cloak and then, with Chrétien's arm about her, they slipped out, unseen, into the night.

KISS AND MAKE UP

Lisette Ashton

According to Descartes," Dracula began slowly, "I think, therefore I am. However, if I think I am a vampire, and we accept that vampires don't exist, does this mean that I don't exist?"

Bob and Linda exchanged a glance.

"What's wrong with him tonight?" asked Bob.

Linda rolled her eyes and shook her head. She cut a striking figure striding by his side. She was tall and raven haired and dressed in a clinging suit comprised of black leather jeans with a matching jacket. Her skin was as white as alabaster except for the full, ripe lips that hid her elongated canines. Bob noticed that Linda's ample chest rose and fell swiftly, as it always did after she had fed. Her long, scarlet nails glinted with slivers of silver moonlight as her fingers twitched impatiently by her hips.

"It's Dracula's dark gift," Linda explained. "Whoever he's been feeding from, he temporarily absorbs some aspect of their personality. When he feeds from drunks, he acts drunk. When he feeds from stoners he gets high." She tossed an impatient glance in Dracula's direction and added, "This is what he gets like after feeding on philosophy students. He'll spend the night being metaphysical and talking incomprehensible bullshit."

Bob nodded and accepted this. He had been feeling a little light-headed himself since feeding and he suspected it was because his victim had been a student.

It had been his idea to visit the student union bar.

Admittedly the necks weren't particularly clean, and most of the victims contained more chemicals than an overstocked pharmacy, but the feeding had been easy, quick and ultimately satisfying. Now, with his bloodlust sated, Bob found his thoughts were moving to different yet more familiar appetites. Staring hungrily at Linda, he licked his lips and graced her with an appreciative smile.

"You've been with Dracula for a while?"

"We've been partners for a couple of centuries," Linda allowed. "Although there are times when it feels longer. Sometimes I think we're just staying together so we can piss each other off and then kiss and make up."

Bob nodded as though he understood. He didn't understand, but he wanted Linda to consider him a good listener so the pretense was essential. He'd read somewhere that women appreciated men who were good listeners and earning Linda's approval was an all-consuming goal that seemed more important than ever now he had fed.

"Dracula doesn't strike me as the most attentive partner," Bob ventured.

Linda shot a scornful glare in Dracula's direction. The legendary vampire was studying the back of his hand with an expression of happy amazement on his face. His violet eyes were wide and incredulous. His lips silently formed the word, *Wow!*

"He's been doing this sort of thing for a long time," Linda sighed. She gestured back toward the cemetery gates, and Bob got the idea she was indicating the carnage they had left behind at the student union bar. Linda's voice was tinged with a mixture of sadness and frustration. "There are times when Dracula forgets that feeding can fuel urges in some of us younger vampires."

"Urges?"

Linda glanced at him. Her eyes were as violet and expressive as Dracula's and they glistened with encouragement. "Strong urges," she murmured.

The trio continued walking through the cemetery. It was a convenient shortcut back to the house they were using as a temporary refuge for their mini-coven. The route was also an apposite reminder of the death they had caused during their feeding frenzy at the SU bar. While Dracula paused and marveled over the "awesome" lichen moss he had found on one ancient headstone, Bob and Linda continued to walk briskly through the moonlit necropolis. Bob noticed that Dracula was falling behind but he kept the observation to himself as he and Linda crunched their way down the gravel path.

"So, feeding fuels strong urges in you?" he prompted.

"Feeding fuels strong urges in *all* us younger vampires," Linda assured him. Her voice had fallen to a husky drawl. "All that biting, feeding and intimacy. Touching strange human flesh. Penetrating bare skin. Tasting blood." She shivered. Her eyes shone. "It's like an appetizer before a meal," she explained. "*Or like foreplay.*"

Bob paused before responding, not sure he could speak without nervousness trembling in his voice. He regarded Linda with solemn appreciation and said, "What's the point of an appetizer if there's no main course to follow?"

"Exactly."

"And what's the point of foreplay if there's no…"

"Exactly," she said again.

With a small giggle Linda snatched at his hand and dragged him away from the cemetery path. The action was so swift that Bob was briefly unsure what was happening. Their feet gave a final scrunch on the gravel before Bob found Linda had dragged him onto a patch of moist grass. She pulled him downward to the discreet shelter behind a tall tombstone. Lying on the grass, she was positioned beneath him with her legs spread wide apart so he could comfortably kneel between them. His body was pressed firmly against hers. The position was so intimate he could feel himself immediately growing hard. His erection throbbed with the sudden prospect of pleasure.

Since becoming a vampire his senses seemed more highly attuned. He was aware of the faraway sound of Dracula stumbling along the gravel path; the distant chirrup of nocturnal insects and birds calling to each other in the night; and the closer scent of Linda's sexual hunger. For an instant he could picture her thoughts: an ability he had come to think of as his own dark gift. In Linda's mind he could see they were both naked, their pallid bodies entwined beneath moonlight on the graveyard grass, and his erection was plunging slowly and solidly into the yielding split of her sex. It was a powerful image and he shut it from his thoughts before Linda could realize he had been reading her mind.

"You do have strong urges, don't you?" he muttered.

"I think we both have strong urges."

She was tugging at the belt that fastened his jeans. On any other woman her long fingernails would have made the task awkward and cumbersome. Linda slipped the belt open with practiced ease and then began to work on the buttons of his jeans, popping them apart with casual dexterity.

"I think we both have the same strong urges," Linda assured him. "And I think we both know how to sate them."

He placed his hand on her wrist, momentarily stopping her from releasing the last of the buttons. "Are you sure this is wise?" Bob asked softly.

"Don't you want to do this?"

He laughed, keeping the sound muted for fear of alerting Dracula to the whereabouts of their hiding place. "I didn't mean that. You know I want to do this as much as you do, but..." He glanced over his shoulder and peered past the shelter of the gravestone.

Dracula continued to stumble down the gravel path. He was now walking with his head held back as he stared at the stars in the sky above. The ancient vampire's face was a mask of childish wonderment. Slowly, he murmured the words, "That is so fucking awesome."

"I mean," Bob told Linda, "what about him? Won't he be pissed off if he catches us together?"

"Damn right he'd be pissed off," Linda agreed. "He'd be absolutely livid." In a conspiratorial whisper that tickled against his earlobe she added, "So we'd best make sure he doesn't catch us." Moving her face from Bob's ear, she placed a kiss against his mouth and slid her tongue between his lips.

Bob made no attempt to resist. He moved his hand from Linda's wrist and allowed her to kiss him with ferocious hunger while her fingers slipped easily into his jeans. Her hands were icy cold—partly from the night's chill and mainly because Linda was all vampire. The cool touch of her fingers against his erection was enough to make him yearn for her with a fresh and furious desire. When her hand encircled his shaft, he had to pull his mouth away from her kiss for fear of the excitement becoming more than he could resist.

"You do have some strong urges, don't you?" Linda whispered.

"As strong as yours," he countered.

Linda's jacket was fastened by a zipper. He pulled it open in one fluid movement to reveal the bare skin beneath. Shadows and darkness kept her body briefly from his view but he traced his hands over the exposed flesh, blindly reveling in the sensation of caressing her naked body.

Linda moaned.

Bob pushed his mouth over Linda's. In an instant the pair were embroiled in a passionate, sultry kiss. As their lips connected, and their tongues wrestled and battled with hungry eagerness, Bob could feel his need for Linda growing more urgent and desperate.

His fingertips brushed over the hard thrust of one nipple.

A spark of electric excitement crackled from his touch.

"Fuck! Yes!" Linda spat.

Encouraged, Bob caught the stiff bead of flesh and teased it firmly between finger and thumb.

The effect on Linda was immediate. She writhed wantonly beneath him. Holding her breast still, so Bob could continue to tease her, she tore at his clothes with animal fury. His shirt was shredded and then wrenched away. Then his jeans were ripped open and tugged downward.

Equally eager to experience Linda's completely bare body, Bob stripped the jacket from her ultrawhite torso. Because they had shifted positions slightly he was afforded his first glimpse of her naked breasts. The sight of her full bosom made his erection throb with renewed urgency. The tips of her nipples were thick and rigid. Their flushed color was almost cherry red against her moonlight pale skin. Unable to resist, Bob lowered his mouth to one breast and sucked hungrily.

Linda stiffened.

And then her loins rose up to meet him. Her body pulsated against his as though they were already in the throes of a more passionate and penetrative act. As Bob greedily sucked and slurped against her nipple he could feel the woman beneath him responding eagerly.

"Fuck me!" Linda grunted. "I want you to fuck me." Her hand returned to his erection and she gripped it with a force that was almost agonizing. "I want you to fuck me now and fuck me hard," she panted. "Do it, Bob."

Bob grinned and began to slowly peel the leather jeans from her hips. If Linda was desperate for him now, he felt sure she would be insane with desire by the time he had slipped the jeans from her legs.

"Quickly," she insisted.

Bob whispered his response while planting lazy kisses against her bare thighs. "I'm going as quick as I can."

"Linda! "

Dracula's plaintive voice echoed from the darkness. He sounded faraway, but not so faraway that Bob thought they could consider themselves safe.

"Hey! Linda!" Dracula called. "Where've you gone, hon? I think I've got lost again."

"Keep quiet," Linda gasped.

Bob hadn't needed the warning. He had no intention of letting Dracula know where they were or what they were doing. He didn't make a sound but simply continued to ease the leather jeans down Linda's strong muscular thighs and plant the occasional kiss against her freshly exposed skin. The scent of her sex had already reached his nostrils. The fragrance of animal need—she was wet and ready for him—was so irresistible he could think of nothing except devouring her. He finally pulled the jeans from her legs and lowered his face to Linda's moist split. Like a connoisseur he marveled briefly over the beauty of her appearance and then gently inhaled her fragrance.

Her natural perfume was intoxicating.

His erection throbbed again and he knew if he simply continued to drink in the scent of her pussy he could possibly reach his climax from that stimulus alone. When he finally lowered his mouth, stroking his tongue against Linda's moist, febrile lips, an orgasmic rush of bliss bristled through his body.

"Fuck!" Linda murmured. "That's good."

"Yes," Bob agreed. He stroked his tongue against her lips again, savoring her rich musk as it tormented his senses.

"Linda!" Dracula called. "Where the hell are you, Linda? I'm getting pissed now."

To Bob, Dracula's distant cries were as meaningless as the night's chill or the collection of freshly drained corpses they had left behind at the SU bar. All that existed for him were Linda's words of encouragement and the sultry sweet flavor of her sex against his tongue. He teased the lips of her labia apart and then trilled the tip of his tongue against her pulsing clitoris. He pushed his tongue between her pussy lips, enjoying the sensation of her inner muscles as they clenched sporadically against him. Her responsiveness was a further joy for him. As Linda trembled beneath him and urged him to continue, Bob couldn't recall a moment when his arousal had felt so powerful or so satisfying.

"Aw! Come on, Linda," Dracula called. "Don't tell me you've gone off screwing that new kid? I thought you said you were done fooling around after I ripped the viscera out of your last conquest?"

Bob slowly pulled his head away from Linda's pussy. His lower jaw glistened with a sheen of her arousal. Linda could clearly see he was unsettled because she placed a reassuring hand on his chest and shook her head. In the softest whisper she said, "Don't listen to him. Dracula didn't rip out anyone's viscera. He's just saying that to try and make himself sound scary."

Bob didn't want to tell Linda that Dracula had succeeded in making himself sound scary. Such an admission was likely to make him appear undesirable and he didn't want to do anything that would spoil the chance of sharing his climax with Linda. Accepting her reassurance, and spurred on by the fact that she was now guiding his erection to her open sex, he forced himself to push his length between her thighs.

There was an instant of pure bliss.

The unvampiric heat of her sex was a furnace around his icy shaft. Her inner muscles gripped his length more tightly than Linda had managed with her strong, powerful hands. As he slid deeper, his length lubricated by a meld of his own saliva and Linda's eager arousal, Bob could feel the climax building in his loins.

Linda pressed her mouth close to Bob's ear and said, "Don't let Dracula worry you with all that talk about ripping out a guy's viscera. It's not true."

Bob was past caring. Sliding in and out of her moist, velvety warmth, he slowed his rhythm so that it matched Linda's steady and relentless motion. His thoughts were occupied only with the divine sensations around his shaft and the determination to stretch their shared pleasure for as long as possible.

Linda shivered beneath him. She jammed a fist into her mouth at one point to stifle a scream of satisfaction. Bob could feel the flood of fresh warm moisture soaking his length as he continued to plough in and out of her sex. When she nibbled lightly on his ear and said, "Fill me with your come," he finally allowed himself the release his body craved.

His length sputtered and pulsed.

A rush of orgasmic relief flooded his body.

Beneath him, Linda groaned with soft satisfaction. She continued to ride her pussy against his pulsing length, milking every last drop of the seed from him and shivering as though his release had been as satisfying for her as it had been for him.

"Linda!" Dracula exclaimed.

Bob stiffened. Cold fingers grabbed his shoulder and then he was torn away from Linda and thrown against a headstone. He caught a brief glimpse of Linda, naked on the grass, her legs spread and a white trickle of his seed dribbling from the spread lips of her sex. And then Dracula was standing over him and fixing him with the most menacing scowl.

"I'll rip your viscera out!" Dracula shrieked.

Linda was struggling to find her clothes. "Don't worry about his empty threats," Linda said quickly. "I told you: he never ripped anyone's viscera out. He's never done that to any of the guys I've played with. All Dracula's ever done was make me help him suck every last drop of blood from the body of the guy I'd been fooling with."

Dracula turned to glare at her.

Bob saw that Dracula's glare became a smile of approval. He was devastated to see Linda return that smile.

"It's almost like one of those bonding exercises they make couples do in marriage counseling," Linda said sweetly. She was talking to Bob but staring directly at Dracula. "I think it allowed us to redevelop our trust for each other again." Her voice had a dreamy quality. "It was like we'd had a chance to kiss and make up and it was so sexual."

"And the guy you were both sucking?" Bob broke in.

Linda shrugged as though the matter was of no consequence. "Just another dead vampire. No creature can survive without having some blood coursing through its veins. Vampires are no exception to that rule."

Dracula grinned and dragged Bob from the ground. "She's right," he confirmed. "No creature can survive without some blood coursing through its veins." His grin grew menacing as he added, "And you're about to find out just how true that is."

Afterward, back at the temporary house, with Bob's drained remains a rotting memory in the graveyard, Dracula turned to Linda and smiled. His lips remained crimson, moist and sultry. "You're going to think I'm depraved," he started. "But ever since we drained Bob, I've been getting urges." He laughed self-consciously and said, "Does that sound depraved to you?"

Linda shook her head. "It doesn't sound depraved. It simply sounds like you're making the most of your dark gift."

He beckoned her with a finger. "Want to help me make the most of my dark gift?"

Linda shook her head. "I'd love to help," she admitted. "But I need to go out before sunrise and recruit a new member for our mini-coven."

A flash of annoyance furrowed his brow. "Already? Can't we go one night without having a third member in our group?" Fixing her with an accusatory glower, he added, "And are you going to fuck this one too?"

She brushed up against him and laughed. "Of course I am," she purred. "If I don't do something to piss you off, we won't have any reason to kiss and make up, will we?" Her fingers brushed against the swell of his thickening erection as she whispered, "And we both know how much fun it is when we have the chance to kiss and make up."

THE STUDENT

Sommer Marsden

A nd here is the Wolff home," he says. "Even the most seasoned paranormal investigators will not go here."

The house is a nightmare behind a chain-link fence, imposing and dark and falling apart.

"Why?" I don't get it. Why would this big-ass spooky mansion be off limits to ghost heads like us, the student body of NAPS? The North American Paranormal Society frowns on avoidance. I tap my pen and wait for our teacher to explain.

"Dread," Mr. Marks says simply. "An overwhelming cold and stony feeling of dread. No one has managed to, uh, soldier on, shall we say? Everyone has turned away, saying it was too intense and real. Too mentally taxing."

"Isn't that kind of wimping out, Mr. M? Isn't that what we're being trained to do? Our institution's not controversial without reason. There are lots of folks pretty pissed that there is a society to train ghost hunters—stalkers of things that go bump in the night." I laugh when he frowns. "So, why wouldn't the investigator just go forward with the investigation?"

He flushes with annoyance. "You're welcome to try and succeed where they have failed, Ms. Marsh." My teacher thinks he's putting the cocky little student in her place.

I shrug. "I might just do that. I'll jot down a paper for you if I do. Give you all the details," I say, as he leads us on up the street. The tour isn't done. This is the most haunted road in Maryland. I stifle a yawn.

"And now that Ms. Marsh is done criticizing, we'll move on to the Borgerding mansion. All of these homes suffered great losses when the factory caught fire and burned. A lot of the bigwigs were trapped when the building collapsed. They owned these homes."

"Unusual," I say to Sam. Sam is to my right taking copious notes per usual. "Usually it's the little guys who die horribly in the fire. Wonder what the bigwigs were doing that they didn't scuttle out like rats leaving a sinking ship."

"Very astute question," says Marks. He's such a sneaky little eavesdropper. "They were having a board meeting on the top floor. The ground floor went up in a wild conflagration."

I have to laugh then. Investigator Marks likes his fifty-cent words. We walk, attentive and shivering in the cold February night up Sparrow's Point Road. "And we're walking," Mr. Marks says just like a cheesy tour guide in a museum. I lean against Sam. Tall and broad, brown eyed and blue haired and hot as hell: even with hair the color of a peacock, I'd fuck him. But he's gay. Sam does not want what I have. "So, you wanna come back with me later tonight?"

"For what?"

"To go through the Wolff house."

"Are you crazy, Helen? Never mind. I know you are." He laughs and shakes his head at me: chicken.

"That's one opinion," I grump and follow the group like a good little learner.

The Wolff house is a holy fucking mess. The front porch is a death trap, rotted boards and sprung nails and six-inch chunks of wood waiting for a fragile foot or exposed bit of skin. "Jesus Christ." The house seems to flinch when I say it. And just like that, there it is, that feeling of dread.

Staggering heaviness descends on me, crushing my lungs, inking out my soul. "God," I sigh. It only gets worse when I utter that name. I want to lie down and die right there on the floor.

I close my eyes and bright white light goes up around me in my mind's eye. I say a prayer of protection in my heart to beings I'm not quite sure I believe in, but it can't fucking hurt, now can it? "Hello?" I yell just to have something to do.

No one answers but I feel the house pause around me. It's like a huge being that has somehow swallowed me whole. "Who's here! I know someone is here. Why are you so sad? Lost? Angry?" I was spitballing it, but I had a recorder going. Maybe on the playback, I'd have a voice, an answer, a whisper.

"Leave." I hear it in my head more than in my ears and my throat wants to close. My lungs want to collapse. My bladder wants to let go.

"You leave!" I force the words out. Thank god I'm such a bitch.

Bitch, hardheaded, stubborn, infuriating, annoying, horrid: every one of these words had been used to describe me. I'm proud of it. I like my reputation. Everyone can be good and follow the rules.

"Now." The voice is a black spot in my brain, a bloody word gashed on the page of my mind in red, red ink.

"No."

A rustle, a blur, the barest of wind and he's on me. I know it's a he, because he is so very, very close I could possibly count the stubble sprouting from the pores of his face. His mouth is latched to my throat and I freeze. My heart is slamming and my head is buzzing. I am somehow crazy enough to notice that my pussy is wet. "I said, leave."

I can feel the threatening sharpness of his teeth over my pulse. "No." I manage. "What are you?"

I know the answer, but I want him to say. The Society has not prepared us for this; ghosts and maybe demons and possibly the Moth Man, sure, but not this. This is legend and movies and Count Chocula Cereal.

Fast—he's fucking fast like a wild thing. In the space of a breath my hands are pinned above my head in one big hand that feels as cold and as strong as a metal manacle. "I'm hungry." That's his answer.

Fear makes my skin slick, my heart skips sickeningly fast. "I can leave now." I want pithy, cocky—I sound breathy and scared. "If you'll just let me go, I'll be on my way." I squirm and he pins me there by pressing my wrists with a fierce frigid strength. His knee forces mine wide and he steps to the very center of me with his thigh. Terror wells up in me but so does a white hot surge of want, need.

"I think I've changed my mind. I think you'll stay. It's been a long time." Press, press, press go those teeth to my throat. In my mind they are long and huge and hooked like a saber-toothed tiger's.

"Since you've eaten?" I snort. It is purely an inappropriate laughter situation, like laughing when someone falls down. I am so scared I feel like I am floating, hovering somewhere above Earth but tethered by his cold dominant grip.

"Among other things. And you're strong. You made it through the front door."

"About that…" I stop because I feel the tip of a fang puncture my skin: penetration. Then there is a thick honey sweetness flooding through my body. A sludge of euphoria in my brain.

"Yes," I whisper. Who said that? I did. I am giving my consent.

That knee pushes harder to spread my legs and he chuckles. My clit is pressed to his immovable thigh and my ever-quickening pulse is a lovely *amuse bouche* under his mouth. Another slice of a millimeter that tooth slides in and the liquid honey travels due south. My pussy thumps in time with my rocketing heart and I hear the breath sigh out of me like I'm dreaming. "Do it," I beg.

Why am I begging to die? I haven't a clue. But part of me is not afraid. Part of me is hospitable to the thought.

Another slip of canine through flesh, another bite of pain, another spark of viscous pleasure. An orgasm rolls through me and I sag in his arms like a doll. "Why are you here?" His demand is like smoke curling into my ear.

"I'm…" Why was I here? What was I doing? Snooping. Breaking rules. Being myself.

More pressure, his fangs sink into my flesh, like a match tip melting into snow. I come again. I float on the dark purple orgasm and shadows flock in my vision like dark crow wings. Am I passing out? Dying? He shakes me like a rag and I hiss— angry, sad, tired.

"Why are you here?" he roars in my ear. His voice is like the ocean rolling onto the beach.

"I'm…I'm a student. Helen. Helen. My name is Helen."

Up comes the thigh and his tongue jumps over the thump of my blood just below my ear. He is tasting me, sampling. He rocks me forward, back, forward, back until little sparkles of what looks like sunshine jump in my vision. Like a sparkler at dusk, writing on the air around me. "The lovely Helen. Like Helen of Troy. How many men have pined for you? How many ships have you launched Helen?"

I come again—how many is that?—and bite my lip to sharpen my focus. "None. I tend to annoy people. And why do you keep doing that? Why do you keep making me come?" I don't really care. It feels good. And if I am going to go out, I want to go out with a bang. Even I, cynic that I am, can see the irony in that.

"You taste even sweeter when you're pleasured." He says it simply, drops my wrists and yanks at my jeans and panties. I hear his zipper and spread my legs for him. I don't ask or question or beg. I simply open for him because that is what I want now. I imagine he will feel like chilled stone.

His hands, cold like river rocks, cup my ass and lift me level. He is icy-cold and hard like the finest marble, a statue come alive, here to rob me of my life and make me so very cold as well. Why am I not afraid?

I wonder if they will find my notebook and recorder or my clothes or bits of me. Will I die here? Will he bury me? Eat me? Drop me in the woods like a used husk?

He slams into me with his long smooth cock and I wrap my legs around his waist, hold on to arms the size of thighs, stare into eyes the color of aged whiskey. Still stunned and dazed and muddy in the head, I slowly realize he isn't feeding now. He's watching me. "You're stunned. I've stunned you. If I let you come out of it, you would be afraid."

I touch his lower lip and he bites my finger. The thick syrupy feeling spreads through me again. I moan as he rocks against me, penetrates, fucks. I move with him, offer him another finger, the middle one. This time I watch his teeth flash, sink, invade and another orgasm turns my brain to blood and sunshine.

"No one ever comes here. They are all afraid. I've made it so." His lips are full and red and I lean in and kiss him. His tongue is as cool as metal.

"I'm too stubborn to be logical."

His cock hits everything, the best and worst of me, slamming deep until my body coils around him, grabbing him with greedy spasms. My nipples ache from the cold of his chest.

"You are brave?"

"Stupid," I correct.

"Curious," he nods. "A warrior."

"Just a student."

His teeth slip along my throat but do not break the skin. He traces my chin with his tongue, brutal thrusts never wavering. His mouth finds my mouth and the insides of his velvety cheeks and the tip of his tongue taste like flowers and watermelon, all things bright and sweet and summertime. I run my tongue over his canine and feel my blood bloom and start to run. He growls—feral, strange. There's a thrill in my blood that he can taste because his teeth, this time, sink all the way home.

"Stay with me."

"I'm a pain in the ass." He fucks me harder and I hear my head banging the wall as if from far away. He tenses and sinks his teeth in farther. He's coming and a noise comes out of his throat like a hiss.

He's overcoming me. He's drinking up my life. It is a dull ache, the kind that touches your bones, like the flu or a break in the bone itself. It floods my body and my mind swirls darker, darker down. "Stay with me," he says again.

"Your name?" What? Why do I care?

"Sebastian. Sebastian Wolff. This was my family home. Stay with me. You taste like youth."

"I'm just a student."

I come one more time but it's weak and pale compared to the others because I'm sinking, losing consciousness. Is this it, or will he bring me back? Does he need permission? My body works the last flicker of orgasm and I cling to him—a moveable mountain with wicked, sharp teeth. His hair is black, I recall. It seems like a hundred years ago that he came tearing into the room for me.

"I can teach you," he says and all I can sense is him now. The world has receded. I'm drowning.

"Do it," I say. And he takes me under.

RED BY ANY OTHER NAME

Kathleen Bradean

Scarlet, crimson, cerise.

There are so many words for red.

He evokes them as a mantra during the long pauses in our telephone conversations. I wonder if he knows that his thoughts spill into my mind.

I turn away from the muted television and snuggle into my couch. He gives good phone.

"May I meet you tomorrow?" His accent is pure American Midwest. Those stocky Wisconsin vowels make me doubt the rumors about him.

He can't truly be undead, the modern part of my brain argues. He can't be a vampire. He's just a sub in search of a domme. My rational mind tries to convince me to calm down, but the other side of my brain screams that his voice is too hypnotic.

I've soaked my panties. What is it about vampire voices? Do they resonate on orgasmic frequencies?

"Don't you dare use your voice or eyes to bring me under

your thrall." This is like scolding a rabid wolf not to bite.

"Please, may I meet you at the club tomorrow?" my vampire asks. This time his voice lacks persuasion. I can tell it's an effort for him to sound human.

This voice doesn't scare me as much. It's not as sexy either. His words don't vibrate down my spine and between my legs.

I shouldn't meet him.

The phone calls I can handle—just barely. I'm not so sure what will happen in person.

"Please."

Cruel inspiration strikes. "Only if you come to me in daylight hours." There, finally, I've set a condition that he can't meet. This will end his pursuit.

I hear traffic. Wind buffets his cellular phone. It's an eternity before he speaks. "That would be difficult." He measures his words.

I wonder what he hears on his end. The hitch in my breath as I hope he says good-bye? My heartbeat? The movement of blood through my veins?

"But I will find a way." He surrenders.

Of course he will. Damn it.

I click off the muted television. "Let's talk about vampire myth versus reality." Despite my fear I'm curious about him.

I put my heels up on the coffee table. My knees spread when I slouch against the overstuffed pillows. There's no way I can hold a rational conversation while my pussy's so engorged.

If he knows that I finger myself while we negotiate, he doesn't mention it.

I lose the thread of our conversation. My thoughts as I hang up the phone are of summer peaches: the aroma of the ripe flesh, the sweet explosion of nectar on my tongue as my teeth break the sun-warmed skin, the rasp of fuzz in the back of my throat.

When I come on my fingers I wonder if those visions were mine or if they were his.

My rational brain says there's no such thing as the undead. As I drive toward the club I almost convince myself that the dead don't walk the night. Still, the side of my brain that controls the steering wheel pulls me into the parking lot of St. Thomas Martyr Church. Here believers in the unknown are offered refuge.

I slip a scarf over my shoulders. I'm not sure if women still have to do that covered hair thing in church or not. Either way I don't want to attract attention. I'm here for insurance, not redemption.

My sunglasses are lowered so I can pretend to read flyers for a firehouse spaghetti dinner fund-raiser and the fifth grade candy bar sale while I hover in the vestibule of the church. My nose wrinkles at the scent of burning wax wafting from the votive candles.

Finally one of the biddies in the front pew remembers an old sin. She shuffles into the confessional, dragging the bored priest in with her. Taking quick advantage, I whip vials out of my purse and submerge them in the font of holy water. Bubbles break the surface as the glass tubes fill. I glance right and left, so obviously guilty of something that I'm surprised no one approaches me.

The manager at the club lets me in, then disappears into his office. The place is deserted.

I change from street clothes to my black latex catsuit in the bathroom. The impossible heels on my lace-up boots change my posture. My copper buttocks thrust out.

According to the full-length mirror on the back of the door, I look hot. Stalling for time, I lean close to my reflection and examine my teeth.

Water drips from a mineral-crusted faucet into the sink on the wall beside me. Hollow echoes sound as each drop falls into a small pool of water ringing the rusty drain.

Garnet, ruby, carnelian.

I know my vampire is close by. Over the phone his thoughts are faint in my mind. Now his voice reverberates along my spine. I look over my shoulder twice to make sure he isn't standing behind me with his lips pressed to the nape of my neck.

All three bathroom stalls are empty.

Beet, tomato, raspberry.

This is his version of fidgeting, I realize. He rattles off his list of reds while he prepares for our session.

I pass the bar on the way to the dungeon I reserved for us. Empty bar stools are set in a meandering line. One has a long gash across the black vinyl cushion. White stuffing puffs out.

Wheezing fans move air-conditioning through the exposed ducts overhead.

Dungeon paraphernalia hangs limp in alcoves. I can see that the black walls of the club need a new coat of paint.

I should have met him at night. More people would have been here. Hesitating, I almost turn to the manager's office.

Strawberry, cherry, candy-apple.

There is a tiny warble in his mental tone. The vampire's nervous about meeting me?

When I open the door he crawls toward me. I doubt his subservience. His emotions splash across my mind. He's the one on hands and knees, but his thoughts are condescending.

The vampire scorns mere humans, but he pursues me, not the other way around. He must be desperate.

As he crosses the concrete floor of the dungeon, his wrists and knees tangle in his brown denim duster. He stumbles.

The dungeon is a small, bleak room furnished with little more than a chair and table. I have no time to consider the rings embedded in the ceiling and walls. My focus is on the creature.

He wears gloves and a hat. His face is swathed in a brown and tan wool tartan scarf. Is he The Invisible Man or a vampire?

"So you can come out in daylight, boy."

He knows better than to answer.

I shove at his ribs with my foot. He obligingly falls over. I straddle him and sit on his chest. I slap him through his scarf. "This is not allowed."

He uncovers his face and I feel a twinge of guilt. He suffers. A fine sheen of pink sweat glistens on his upper lip. His sweat has a faint reptilian tang.

My full weight is on his ribs. My pubic hair presses against his coat. His eyes flicker down to the cutout in my catsuit that exposes my crotch. I lean close to his face. He has freckles!

"You came out in daylight," I praise him.

"It is possible," he admits. He breathes calmly. My weight is nothing to him.

Maybe breathing is an affectation for a vampire. Why would the dead need air?

"Will you be okay?"

My concern triggers an alien response in his mind that I can't fathom. Is he insulted or touched?

"I will not be completely comfortable until darkness falls, but I can endure it."

I slap his bared cheek with my gloved hand. "Then take off the damn clothes, boy."

Underneath the coat and scarf and layers of other protections, he wears chinos and a golf shirt. No capes or tuxedos for my vampire.

There is the air of autumn to him, wholesome as hayrides

and apple cider, yet tinged by winter cold.

His thick blond hair is sun-kissed in wide streaks. I wonder if the tan on his chest will fade.

His hands ball into loose fists. He waits for me to make a joke about his white-bread, country-club looks.

Instead, I draw a knife lightly across the bend of my elbow. A thick, warm trickle snakes down my forearm.

He stops, pant fly unbuttoned and unzipped, light blue briefs showing. He lifts his nose slightly, moves it barely right and left. His nostrils spread wide as he scents me in the air.

He transforms into a pure predator. There is nothing human in his eyes.

My hand goes to my whip resting on the small table. "Finish undressing now," I growl.

I will not fear, I remind myself. I must not fear. Fear is the little death, the mind killer. Where did I learn that quote? The little death. *La petite mort.* Every orgasm is a little death. Death and sex, that beast with two backs. My mind is free associating in hysterical bursts. I must not fear. Fear will be the death of me.

Burgundy, wine, claret. This is his mantra to keep control. Red drinks, I notice. It may have been a mistake to tempt him with blood.

He kneels. He knows the proper postures, the right responses. This is not new to him.

I whip his naked flesh. He pretends to flinch but I know that he's bored. Normally my strokes have to be pulled. For him I put my back into it and I grunt with the delivery. He feels no fear, no real pain, no submission.

Even though his eyes are supposed to be on the ground, he tilts his chin so that his peripheral gaze is on my open wound.

He patiently allows me to bind his arms and legs. It amuses him to obey my terse commands.

"Are there no vampire tops?" He's beyond human help.

"Do you know any other vampires besides me?"

"No."

"Neither do I. Not anymore." He turns away from me deliberately. His wrists twist. The leather bonds fall away, torn in two.

I'm defeated. His physical strength and tolerance for pain mock me. There's nothing I can give him.

Sinking into the master's chair, I spread my thighs.

"Come, boy."

He moves in a blur, a gliding motion that I can't quite see. Until now he's acted as human as possible for my sake.

He licks the inside of my thigh. The very tip of his thin tongue is bifurcated, forked. Crouched, he spreads my labial lips and considers my offering.

He uses his thumb on my clit.

I start to correct him, but his tongue explores my groin at the top of my thigh. I relax back into the chair. The sensation is new. I wonder what other tricks he knows.

There's a main artery that passes near the inside of the thigh. I remember that from some class I once took. Then I wonder why that trivia came to my mind.

His crafty tongue dowses my pulse. His fangs press against the skin over it. Not the points, but the flat, smooth surfaces of his elongated canines. He pants.

I'm thinking about something, I remind myself, something I should worry about.

He slaps my clit.

There's something important I need to focus on, something other than the heat that rushes between my legs.

I spread my legs farther apart to let him in closer. Wicked flashes of forbidden thoughts dart through my brain. I chase those images through dark labyrinths.

My body is warm from my toes to the top of my head. I couldn't rise from this chair if I wanted to.

He suckles my skin. He wants to merge with me.

I shouldn't let him. He has far too much control of this scene. I'll put him back in his place—in just a moment—I'm almost there—another moment.

Time ebbs.

No, I have to take back control right now. I can't help him if I let him top me.

At some point I closed my eyes. Now I struggle to open them. The exposed fluorescent lights on the ceiling are harsh. My eyelashes flutter like moths beating their wings against a bulb.

This is wrong. I have to open my eyes and look. It's like swimming through thick water. I'm drowning in lust. It's not my eyes that need focus, it's my brain. I fight to surface into reality.

We share an emotion. It wells inside me, inside him: need. My pussy thrusts for his mouth. The shared hunger grows, overwhelms me.

I'm wet, slick wet. He penetrates me. I grind into his hard—

He's feeding!

Adrenalin snaps me into full awareness.

I grab his hair and pull him off me.

He snarls. Blood coats his teeth. Thick red smears across his pale face.

I hit him hard, harder than I've ever dared hit anyone before. I catch his chin with force. He barely turns aside, and then smiles. He delicately licks the pool of blood at the corner of his lips.

"You will be punished for that." I shake. I know what bloodlust feels like now. And worse, I know how good it feels to sate it.

He doesn't care. He thinks that he can take anything he wants from me.

"Assume your position."

He smirks but drops down so that his cheek touches the cement floor.

I grab one of my vials of holy water. My gloves make unscrewing the cap a desperately unfunny comedic scene, but it finally pops off. I tip the tube. One tiny drop splashes down on his exposed backside.

He yelps.

Pain, he's feeling real pain for the first time in ages. It repulses yet fascinates him.

I sink back into the master's chair. My legs press tight together. I drag him over my lap.

He tries to wriggle away.

Another drop falls on his backside. He screams. Two welts rise.

"This is what happens to bad boys. Feeding without permission earns you ten drops."

I caress his buttocks. The next drop of holy water lands between his shoulder blades.

This reminds me of a good caning—the catch of the breath as the stroke falls, then the lip bitten to muffle a sob.

The fourth drop makes him suck air in between his clenched teeth. He's beginning to remember fear. He worries that the throbbing pain across his back will never fade.

Parting his asscheeks, I stroke his anus.

He's engorged. His pale face flushes under the drying blood. Lifting his ass with his strong thighs, he grinds against my leg.

Drops five, six, and seven fall in fast succession.

Vampires can cry. They have pink tears. He sobs. He begs for my forgiveness.

I let him anticipate the eighth splash of holy water. He breathes heavily and postures while he braces.

I force him back down to the floor. He spreads his knees and arches his back.

His back is mottled with welts. They will heal slowly. Every movement he makes now betrays stiffness in his muscles. Yet, as he presses his face into my mound, pleased purrs sound from in his throat.

His long, thin tongue explores inside me.

It tickles, it caresses. I can't decide if I like it or not, but my body has other ideas and soon my hips rise to meet him.

I can feel his laughter. That's good too. Everything inside me rumbles back and ooh—it feels delicious.

He braces my thighs apart and lifts my ass from the chair. He's strong enough to do that.

I grab his head and press him deep into me.

His freckled button of a nose rubs into my clit. I throw myself against it. Every touch brings a twinge of pleasure.

I'm soaked in my juices.

He gulps in my scent.

Heat radiates off me. I sweat underneath my latex. The sharp odor of my perspiration rises in the air. I grasp at the red crushed-velvet arms of the master's chair. My fingers try to slide between my legs, but he is there. He is everywhere inside me.

His straight locks are just long enough to pull. I dig my fingers into that mane. He grunts as I rip some out by the roots.

His thumb slides into my ass and his tongue fills my pussy. I'm not sure who's rewarding who, but my only clear thought is that I'm filled and it's incredible.

I gasp. Pre-orgasmic heat glows from my cheeks and lips. Against my throbbing clit, he flicks the tip of that extraordinary tongue. I can feel myself crest a wave that breaks and rolls into intense primal pleasure.

Rojo, rouge, rosé.

Now he speaks in tongues.

My heart pounds through my chest, my anus clenches his thumb, and my pussy milks his tongue.

I lock my thighs around his head. His lips seal around my clit. He suckles my juices.

Tiny tremors of delight ricochet through me, the ebbing wave of my orgasm.

He dares to raise his eyes to see if I am pleased. I tip the vial again, pouring out a measure equal to four of the previous drops. I swear I can hear it sizzle as it meets his skin.

At first he howls. As he writhes he thinks the safeword. I hesitate. Does that mean I should stop the scene? Does he know I can hear his thoughts?

His focus moves within.

Our minds link. I am drawn inward with him.

The pain follows him. There is no escape.

The tension flees the knotted muscles across his slim back as he surrenders.

Beyond his pain, free from his unnatural nature, he finds peace. He finds relief. He desperately wants this reconnection to his lost humanity. He craves it.

I stand on wobbly legs.

He presses his face to my boot. He rubs his cheeks and forehead across the leather. I lift my toe. He kisses the sole.

Now I'm on familiar ground. I understand him. We have entered my domain, my area of expertise. I know what I can give him.

His thoughts envelop me. *Carmine, cardinal. Pomegranate, vermilion, maroon.* Contented thoughts buzz through his brain and into mine like lazy late-summer bumblebees. His heavy-lidded eyes close to half slits.

I plan a future of garlic-infused flails and silver-plated cock rings.

He indulges in a connoisseur's litany: *sangre, anima, blood.*

ENLIGHTENMENT

Amber Hipple

Once, I loved the night. I would stalk through the darkness, feeling as if I were somehow *more* than in the sunlight. The darkness was a time for adventure and this feeling remained with me even into adulthood. Now, the lights of the city are so bright they fill the sky, turning the night into dusk and banishing the stars from my sight. The night was once a deep velvet cloak that settled over everything, bathing it in a sweet mystery that could not be captured when the sun was up. It was easier to dream and fuck and love under the veil of night. It was easier to live then.

There is no modesty, no trepidation, when no one can see your face. You are your words and your actions. You can be your essence. And so there is a bravery that comes from this. There is a recklessness born from anonymity, and a release from fear. I miss being that wild creature, that thing of daring and boldness that welcomed the mask.

Now the city is too bright. We have forgotten mystery, no

longer seem to need it or want it. Everything must be clear and bright. This is just another way to banish fear. To know those things that were mysterious gives us power, but also takes from us a sense of wonder. So the light flares and the only place to find darkness is behind our closed eyes.

When I lie down, letting my heavy lids slide over my eyes, that black comes back and envelops me. I feel as if I am floating. I welcome this. There again is the sense of freedom that I found on darkened streets and in night-filled parks. There again is that sense of awe and excitement that the unknown has always brought. I close my eyes and I can dream.

Not half-baked sleeping dreams, but vivid waking dreams that come when you hover on the cusp. That time, like all cross-roads, holds a magic all its own. This place behind my eyes has now become his place. This is when he comes, and I welcome this stranger, seeing in him the things I long for and the things I would return to.

He is a secret longing. His long hair is dark and smooth as oiled silk. It wafts around him like the halo of a fallen angel or the flare of some black sun. He smells of cedar and spice. His obsidian skin is like glass, hard and smooth. He has been chipped from the stone, all planes and angles. He is sharpness that gouges at my questing fingertips and hungry lips. His eyes draw me deeper and deeper, until I feel I cannot breathe, but in his embrace it does not matter.

He wraps me in his words. My longing's voice is a satin bass that strokes the delicate hairs of my ear and tickles in a way that is *yes* and *no*. Dark things insinuate themselves into my mind. He whispers of death and pain. He speaks to me of hidden secrets: fire and midnight purple phoenixes and philosopher's stones. He promises to teach the alchemy of his soul and usher me into a life at his side where each night would be more exquisite than the last. He calls me his tortured darling and speaks to secret desires. These words are like soft touches against my skin and my spine. Let him speak to me till I turn to dust in his arms.

My creature, my desire...he is black against black. Only those words and his touch tell me when he is near. I feel him, like electricity, raising the tiny hairs on my arms. He is a bringer of pain, primitive and thoughtless, touching raw nerves and bringing my senses awake. Beneath my hands and covering me, he is feverishly warm, a lightless fire. His sinful lips send lightning twitching through my limbs. Hurting, tingling, aching, burning, my body begs for more of those touches and kisses that leave me trembling and gasping.

I stand in nothing, blackness. I feel air, warmth and fear. His voice is a caress that teases me from behind, stirring the fine hairs on my neck. "Victoria." The fear is gone. I know this creature, my dream. I have touched him, tasted him, and though I know him to be wild and predatory, I know too that he awakens this in me. To fear him is to fear myself. A hand traces down my side, lingering on my hip.

"You," I breathe and turn to him, toward the feel of him, and am rewarded with his lips against mine. I will speak no other words this night. I have no need. My dream's lips slide down my neck and over my shoulders. I feel his teeth nipping at my skin. Immediately there is a buzz that begins in the back of my head, a drone that loosens my body. And there is a want that grabs hold, beginning as a knot in my stomach. I grip his shoulders.

I see a flash of white teeth. He grins before dark hair obscures my vision. I am laid back. Large hands stroke over my ribs and I feel his mouth on my breasts. Shock moves me, all the way to my toes. I arch toward him, and he laughs. "So eager," he says. My response is only a moan. His lips brush over the soft skin of my tummy and now my fingers slide into his thick hair.

He works his way down my body with those wondrous lips, and stops at the delta of my thighs, inhaling. "So sweet," he murmurs. My mystery has a tongue dark as he, and forked. I feel that slippery serpent tongue, agile, surrounding my clit. My hips twitch, grinding my cunt up against his mouth, and I grip his hair harder.

That tongue slips through my folds, licking me with feathery flickering touches. He tugs and pulls and prods me close to orgasm, always stopping just short until I am maddened and begging. Then, his tongue seeks into me, probing and twisting. I breathe hoarsely now. He holds my hips while his tongue dances, keeping me close while he denies my release. My body trembles and my thighs clench. I want nothing except to be filled.

But still, I am denied, sulky, bitter, and afire; he must pull me up with cruel hands while he laughs. My skin lies against his; I feel the fire of him, the hard length of his body and his throbbing cock against my thigh. "Touch it," he says, and guides my hand. It's smooth, cool, jumping against me, when I touch him. I squeeze and run my thumb over the head of his cock, slicking it with the precum that has gathered there. My stomach flutters. *I want.* Kneeling, I take him into my mouth. My mystery's head lolls back, strands of hair whispering against his thighs. I hear him exhale slowly and deeply, as if trying to retain control.

With his hard fingers in my hair and his skin standing out against my ivory pallor, he moves himself into my throat. He tastes of cinnamon. I work his shaft with my tongue and let my teeth slide so gently against the head of his cock. This is living stone forcing its way past my lips. I work him with my hands as well and his breathing deepens. My dream's hips begin to buck as he thrusts himself harder and faster. There is no longer any artifice. I suck in earnest, wanting his release and burning with a need for fulfillment that I know only comes after his. I choke on his engorged cock and onyx tears leak from the corners of my eyes, falling warm and hard. Moaning, urging wordlessly, I feel his cum sear my throat like whiskey and bathe my chest like ice. My limbs are numb with the remembrance of his thrusts and his cum hardens into spiderwebs in my blonde hair.

We breathe. I hear him, smell him, and feel him, as he kneels with me. My thighs are slick and coated. His hand slips between my legs, sliding against my cunt, and without urging I lie back. I feel his palms move to my knees, moving my legs apart. He thrusts, filling me. My body jumps, I cannot help it. I am full and I moan. I feel every inch of my incubus pressing against my walls, pressing against the back of me.

I feel his thrusts in my marrow. He pounds against me in a counterbeat to my heart. His hips beat against mine. My body accepts him; my lips beg for more. This friction is the distillation of freedom. This is freedom to live, to enjoy, to love as I choose and not from fear. I am nothing but myself here as he batters himself against me. It is sweet.

Leaning forward, he cups my breasts. Nipping teeth draw blood from my nipples. My sinner, my dream, he drinks from my breasts. Suckling as a man, drawing moans from me. As his tongue and teeth pull at my breasts, those hips continue to pound at me relentlessly. I feel overwhelmed. Pleasure prickles at every cell in my body. I cannot form rational thought. When he whispers in my ear, tells me to come, I do.

Violent and harsh, my voice leaves my throat raw. My

back arches upward and I press my body to his, clutching the smooth strong planes of his back while my body quivers. My cunt spasms around him, clenching him tight. His nails, sharp as razors, stroke my back and bring thin lines of blood that I cannot feel as I am still lost in the tide.

Euphoria suffuses me so that at first I do not notice that he has gone. I curl on my side, pressing my thighs together to try and prolong the sensations of orgasm. As the cloud of pleasure fades, my heart cries. He has left me. I could reach out my arms, try to capture him and hold him to me but already I know it is pointless. He is no longer something I can hold.

My lover has become tendrils of smoke that move over my body like soothing fingers. These vines of black smoke wreathe and bind me as sure as his hand and arms do. They flicker over me, healing the stinging wounds on my back and easing the soreness that he brings to my limbs. I cry now, for the gentleness that he is showing me.

There is no shame in my tears, no embarrassment. I cannot see him, smoke and mirrors, but I could not see him before. There is no judgment in the dark, with the dark. I can be only myself. So I cry for the tenderness I feel in these gentle ephemeral touches. When my body begins to sing with renewed pleasure, the touches are gone. I am alone in my night, still weeping for something that I lost. I find it again when I dream, but each night it ends. It hurts to be alone, alone in my dreams and alone in the concrete brightness of the city. He is a dream.

Eventually, true sleep claims me. I wake to dried blood, crusty on my skin. I stand in front of the mirror and examine the new lacework pattern of scars on my back. Sweeping my hand over my white sheets, smoothing them, I find the small teardrop bit of onyx. Stark and black against the white, it glitters. I palm it, almost burning myself, and place it with the others. Soon, I will have enough to make something. I imagine a scintillating gown and clothing myself in pieces of the night. Perhaps I can keep him closer to me. Perhaps then I may have him and have the creature that is myself, always, and not just in the darkness.

BLOOD AND BOOTLEG

Teresa Noelle Roberts

Connecticut, 1922

"Daddy, what is that...that *Hun* doing in this house?"

Lily managed to keep her voice to an indignant whisper, but she swore the tall, icily blond object of her wrath turned and stared at her across the ballroom.

She shuddered.

The horrid creature had been giving her the glad eye all night long, along with half the men at the party and at least one girl who was enjoying Vassar in a very special and intimate way.

As if she'd mess around with a German.

There was something creepy about the way he stared at her with those pale, intense blue eyes.

Creepy in a way that would have been intense and sexy coming from a different man.

"We're doing business together, sweetheart. Wouldn't do not to invite him to the party. And I'm pretty sure he's been in this country since...eighteen-eighty-something. No, can't be.

He's too young for that. Before the war, anyway." Mr. Swift's Alabama drawl was more pronounced than usual. He'd been drinking a lot then.

Lily sighed. Not that she wasn't a bit spifflicated herself. Daddy's money assured that they had real contraband champagne, not speakeasy swill, and she was taking advantage of it. But once Alabama got the better of Daddy's years in Connecticut, reason wouldn't get anywhere.

Still, she had to try—for Harry's sake.

"Today of all days you had to invite a German to our house? It's bad enough you're throwing a party today, but inviting him here is too much."

"It's your birthday." He wasn't just drawling. He was slurring. "Party's for you. Go have fun."

If only it were that easy. Twins belonged together, but hers was dead and no one seemed to understand that part of her had died with him. Oh, she'd pretend to have fun, and maybe succeed for a little while if she got drunk enough or found the right man. Bad behavior took her mind off the blackness.

But not for long. "It's Harry's birthday too. And he's dead because of someone like that tuxedoed monster." He didn't even die in Flanders fields where he'd be considered a hero. No, he made it home and died, horribly, here.

A shadow passed over her father's usually jovial face. "Don't you think I remember that? I miss your brother every day. Just like I miss your mama." He took another drink of the neat bourbon he favored. "Seems cold to go on sometimes, but we don't have a choice in that. Not a good choice anyway. Figure those Catholics have it right about killing yourself. God hates waste. Or maybe He hates the competition. Wants to do the job Himself."

Her father stared off into the distance, either surrendering to his thoughts or looking for a waiter to get another drink. Either way, she'd lost him for the moment, though, ironically, she felt closer to him than she had since Harry finished coughing up his mustard-gassed lungs and found peace from his nightmares.

She shook herself. If she kept on at this rate, she'd be seeing one of those awful Freudians again, or worse. Lily forced herself to grab another champagne. Getting pie-eyed beat getting misty-eyed about what couldn't be changed.

Beat thinking about the Hun in the corner, staring at her with pale, hungry eyes.

Beat admitting to herself that before she heard his accent, she'd been ready to use him as this evening's distraction. Dancing and drinking could stave off the blues for a while, and riding or driving fast and hard worked during the day, but nothing built a wall between her brain and the memory of her brother's slow, awful dying like a little nookie with some handsome sheik. And this one made her knees weak and her peach silk tap pants damp, with his high cheekbones and fair hair that clung to his head like pale gold satin, and his tall, well-made body.

His shoulders were almost too broad to look elegant in an evening suit, despite the best efforts of an obviously expensive tailor. But that just meant he'd look better naked.

The thought of the German bared and ready to impale her on his cock like he was stabbing her back to life instead of to death made her shudder with need.

And it made her angry enough that the next mental image was of marching through the crowd and slapping his damn sculpted Germanic face hard enough all the chatter would cease and even the jazz band would stop playing as the report echoed around the room.

Not a good idea. It would fox her father's latest wheeling and dealing and she'd get her allowance cut off...again. After the last time, her favorite stores, not to mention her favorite bootlegger, would be less eager to extend her credit.

Might be a good time to calm herself down before she did something stupid, as opposed to just plain screwy. People expected screwy from her, and Lily was glad to oblige. Beat getting all grummy and crying in the dark.

But right now the press of people was grating on her last nerve and she still wanted to hit the Hun. The night air might do her some good.

Clutching her drink, she slipped toward the French doors, shrugging off hands, ignoring cries of "Lily! Lily darling!" from former and would-be lovers.

On the veranda, she could still hear strains of jazz and occasional peals of laughter, just enough to tease her ears annoyingly until she wandered into a wild, overgrown area of the garden.

She'd always liked being out here in the dark. She'd never brought a beau here, though it had a lot of privacy for necking and nookie. It was her place, not to be shared. Not with anyone except Harry, who'd understood.

Peace at last.

Only being in the mood she was in, distance from the party that had been driving her crazy made her feel lonely instead of peaceful. It reminded her how alone she was. She'd been born one of two, and even when Harry had been in the trenches half a world away they hadn't really been apart.

Now she'd always be lonely, no matter how many people she surrounded herself with or how many men she fucked.

A large male hand clasped Lily's bare shoulder. "You are hurting, I think. Perhaps I can help."

The voice, deep and growly in the most erotic way, sent excitement rippling through Lily.

A hint of something foreign and exotic made it even sexier,

even though she recognized the accent immediately as German.

Lily wheeled around.

He smiled one of those deliciously world-weary European smiles.

The damn Hun was sex incarnate.

No. She wouldn't. She couldn't.

And that meant she had to get him away from her, because she'd had enough champagne that she'd do something regrettable if he stayed in flirting range.

"You can help by going to hell. Or at least getting out of my house."

She swung at him, but the German grabbed her wrist and yanked her against his body.

He smelled like vetiver and spice, and underneath it, like pure man. It went to her head and her fury dissipated.

She looked up at him, realized he was about to kiss her.

And German or not, she was going to let him.

The kiss, when it came, was brutal enough to make Lily remember wartime headlines screaming about "The Rape of Belgium" but this was sensual brutality, brutality with raw erotic power behind it, and it threw her from brooding and into the moment.

His teeth scraped her lips, her tongue. They seemed sharper than the common run, but the hint of pain helped focus her, keep her out of the gray place she'd been slipping into. She thought she might be bleeding. She didn't much care.

"I am not your enemy," the man said when they paused for breath. "I took no part in this foolish war that cost your brother's life. I left my homeland many years ago, so many that now I have no wish to go back."

There was so much sorrow in his voice that Lily suspected it was more that he couldn't go back. "Who are you?" she asked.

And then some instinct she didn't understand prompted her to ask, "What are you?"

He bowed neatly. "An interesting question. I am called Johann von Bayern. As for what I am, perhaps I am your salvation, Fräulein Swift. Perhaps I am your damnation."

"Or perhaps you're an arrogant older man who thinks he can pick up a girl with fancy talk." She smiled her best flirtatious smile. "And maybe you can. At least if you swear you weren't involved in the war."

"Oh, I swear. I have seen far too much blood and death to wish to ever fight again. The last war I fought in was your American Revolution, and before that the Hundred Years' War."

She gave his broad chest a playful shove. "So you're a joker as well as a smooth talker? Or someone told you I'd majored in history and you wanted to see if I knew my onions."

"I do not jest."

"Jeez Louise, I'm sorry I said you were older. I just meant you're older than me, not that you're ancient."

"Thank you, but I *am* ancient. Older than you can imagine. I was born in the year of our Lord 1162, Fräulein. I fought many battles even before the Hundred Years' War."

Either this guy was better than Buster Keaton at the deadpan face or he was a lunatic. Lily was hoping for the first option, even if he sounded serious as cancer. Crazy wasn't good for what she needed. She needed someone sexy and fun but sane to distract her from her own craziness. Neurotic or depressed or whatever her Freudian called it before she'd thrown a book at him and fled, but *crazy* would do.

Only one way to be sure about Johann: play along. "So, what are you? You're too solid to be a ghost. A vampire, maybe?" She and her college roommates had read *Dracula* out loud to each other, enjoying the pleasant scare and giggling about how it was all a metaphor for sex.

Johann smiled, but it wasn't the smile of someone who was actually amused. Cold and predatory, a cat's smile, it made her want to shrink away. But at the same time, it made her want to draw closer—to wipe it off his face and make him smile for real. "You recognize me. I am humbled. But I am not surprised. You crave darkness, whether you know it or not. Your pain cries out to me, Fräulein. Perhaps I can ease your pain, and you my loneliness."

He drew her closer as he spoke. His voice rang with conviction and age-old sorrow.

He was not a kidder; delusional, maybe.

That should have scared her off.

Instead it attracted her. If he was delusional, it was likely because of the war—think about what he'd said about blood and death. A lot of soldiers came home uninjured, but not right in the head. And which side he'd fought on suddenly didn't matter. He'd been caught in a war that hadn't been his idea and it had left him with a hollow place inside he'd filled up with wild fancies.

Lily understood that hollowness all too well.

Besides, back at college, her friends had voted her first to die if a vampire ever hit campus, because she couldn't resist a thrill or a smooth-talking sheik.

She had to ask herself what kind of trouble she was about to get herself into.

The usual kind, she told herself, the kind that would keep her, one more night, from slitting her wrists.

And if it wasn't the usual kind? If Johann was dangerous, not just sad and peculiar?

The surge of fear blended with a surge of arousal, hot and

wet and overwhelming, so she couldn't have said exactly why she was shaking in his arms.

She didn't try to pull away, though.

"Does it matter?" Johann asked as if he read her thoughts through her trembling body. "You fear death and yet you crave it. You crave life and yet you fear it. Whether I end your torment through ecstasy or extinction, it matters little to you."

"How did you...?" She didn't know how to ask the question.

"I smell the fear and the lust coursing together in your blood. I know your pain, Fräulein Swift. And I know what you need."

Men always said that, and usually they hadn't a clue.

But Lily had a feeling that Johann knew from his own school of hard knocks. He'd read her like a book—and a book with small words and big pictures at that.

"I know what you need," he repeated. She felt his hard cock tease her body through their clothes. "May I give it to you?"

So polite for a madman—and so very sexy.

"Yes," she said, embarrassed that her voice came out as a schoolgirl squeak.

Big hands ripped her dress, leaving her naked to the night except for tap pants, garters and stockings.

She wanted to protest. The violence of his desire hardened her nipples and surged into her clit but she'd loved that dress, and besides it was going to make it hard to get back inside.

But Johann lowered her to the grass, laying her down on his jacket and straddling her body and she couldn't find words, didn't want to find them.

When had he gotten undressed? She must be more ossified than she'd realized if she'd missed that, but the sight of him naked and kissed by moonlight removed any doubts she had.

What kind of "business" was he doing with her father, anyway? He dressed beautifully and talked like an educated man but he hadn't gotten arms and thighs like that sitting at a desk or playing tennis and golf. Those were bulky muscles, the kind a fella got from manual labor. (Or sword-fighting, she couldn't help thinking. Not that he'd really been born in the Middle Ages, but she could imagine him in armor, or taking it off to despoil captive-maiden Lily.) And Lily wanted him inside her more urgently than she remembered ever wanting a man inside her before.

She reached for his erection, but he caught her hand and held it out to the side with an ease that made her clench. "Patience."

"Not my middle name," she managed to say.

"It is mine, however. An advantage of my great age."

She wanted to tease back, because that must have been teasing, but when he closed his mouth over one tight nipple and cupped her sex through peach silk, she couldn't say anything except "Please," and then "Oh, Johann, yes!"

No one had ever handled her like this before. His touch through the silk was exquisitely gentle, bringing her to the brink of release and holding her there deliberately. At the same time, he savaged her nipple, suckling hard, then biting down hard. It should have hurt. Between the way he was teasing her clit, and the wild cocktail of desire and nerves already intoxicating her (not to mention the champagne), though, it felt as though the edge of exciting pain was going to release the shadows in her head.

She whispered, "Harder. I don't care if I bleed, as long as I don't think."

"That is my notion."

He bit harder, and it felt like hot needles piercing into her flesh, but in a good way.

She yelped, from surprise as much as pain. It hurt, but he was sucking and tonguing her nipple and the strong sensations from that turned the pain into rough pleasure. He suckled with determination, as if he were drawing nourishment from her like a baby, but what he was drawing from her was pleasure.

And that haunted feeling she'd lived with since Harry died.

And maybe some blood, because he raised his head once and smiled at her in the moonlight and she swore his lips were redder than they had been, the skin around them stained.

A little freakish, given he was convinced he was a vampire, but what was a little broken skin if it felt that good?

He lowered his face to her other breast and bit again. At the same time he circled his fingers just right, just where she needed them. As pain and pleasure mingled, she dug her fingernails into Johann's shoulder, drawing blood in turn, and came hard enough that the night spun around her.

"Now," she whispered, because that was all she could articulate.

"This is truly what you want?" His voice was a growl and Lily could tell he was being a gentleman by sheer will, that what he wanted to do was thrust into her like a savage.

Luckily that was what she wanted too. "Yes," she managed. "Take me." Forget French letters; she'd take her chances this time.

Johann ripped her tap pants off as easily as he had her dress. "So wet," he whispered, stroking her for the first time without cloth intervening, bringing her to the brink of orgasm again. "So alive. I feel your blood pulsing in your clit, Lily."

He moved then, pressed his mouth between her legs—and bit down on her clit, hard.

Yikes. Did Johann sharpen his teeth in keeping with his vampire obsession? She managed to stifle the yelp of pain.

But not the scream of pleasure when he swirled his tongue on the aching flesh and drew another orgasm from her.

She was still contracting when he entered her, hard and rough and perfect. Lily wrapped her legs around his hips, pulling his cock even deeper inside her. He was pounding against the mouth of her womb and like much of what he'd done it was slightly painful and intensely pleasurable at the same time.

She bit down on his shoulder and tasted copper.

"Sorry about that, Johann. Lost control of myself. You're bleeding," she said, and licked at the wounds her teeth and fingernails had made.

"So are you, Lily."

Then he laughed aloud and his fangs glinted in the moonlight.

His big, sharp fangs.

Holy god, he wasn't a lunatic. He was a vampire.

Lily knew how Mina and Lucy in *Dracula* must have felt. She ought to fight him or scream, hit him with a rock, start praying, something.

But the vampire was fucking her like a genius and she couldn't do anything but ride the bliss and buck against his body, frantic to come again despite her panic.

A desperate laugh bubbled out of her throat. "Figures...after a few centuries a man would know what he's doing."

"Hush, Lily," he said, his voice almost tender.

He flexed his hips, drove deep inside her again. Pleasure curled out from where their bodies joined. It felt like moonlight filling her, silvery and magical, and it shattered some of that hard guilt and sorrow she'd carried with her for so long. Tears streamed down her cheeks, but for the first time in years they were tears of release, not grief. She rippled around him, felt his cock jump with the force of her orgasm.

Johann paused in midthrust and kissed her on the forehead, as gently as her father might. "You've tasted the ecstasy. Now it's eternity or extinction, Lily. You choose."

He sighed, an ancient sound that made more sense to Lily's pleasure-addled brain than his words did.

Then he ripped out her throat.

It didn't hurt after the first shocking pain, but she must have blacked out briefly.

When Lily became aware again, Johann was holding her in his lap, one hand caressing her blood-spattered hair, the other working between her legs still, like a man who'd let loose sooner than he'd wanted to but had the courtesy to make sure his girl was pleasured. She couldn't feel anything except a distant, sweet pressure, though.

I'm dying. But what a way to go.

Not the sex. That had been great, but not worth dying for. But this sense of peace was. She couldn't hold on to that serenity if she lived but it was worth dying for a few minutes when everything was as it should be. No more pain. No more fear. No more sorrow.

And the man—the vampire—who'd killed her was weeping red tears for her.

"Don't cry," she tried to say, although all she could do was mouth the words.

Then blackness wiped out the moon and Johann's face.

"You goof!" a familiar voice exclaimed. "I've never minded you tagging along, Lily, but enough is enough."

She couldn't find her body anymore, but she knew she was smiling. "Harry!" She couldn't see his face in the brilliant golden light that embraced them both, could barely make out his lanky form, but she'd know that voice in heaven or in hell.

A quick, hard embrace—and then a shove. "Go back, Lily. The afterlife's pretty keen, but I missed out on a lot by dying young. You need to live for both of us."

"You've been calling to me...."

Harry laughed, and it was his old laugh from before the war, when his lungs and his throat and his soul were all unscarred. "I was trying to tell you to cheer up. I still feel what you feel, Sis, like we always did, and your miseries aren't much better than what I put you through when I was dying. But feel this."

Harry kissed her. It wasn't a brotherly kiss, and she realized that her awful Freudian probably had a point with some of his nastier insinuations. Maybe she had been seeking Harry in other men's arms, because kissing him felt like coming home.

And then her heart filled up with giggly golden joy.

"Do you feel that? That's what being alive is, if you let yourself feel it. And the only way I can feel it again is if you do. So go and live. For both of us."

Another shove—and Lily sputtered and coughed and opened her eyes to cold moonlight and Johann's astonished face.

"You seemed to crave death so much, but you chose life. You must have tasted enough of my blood…"

Lily touched a hand to her throat. It was whole, smooth, unscarred. There was no pain, and it wasn't because she was in shock this time.

There was no pain inside either, only a memory of the golden joy Harry had shared with her.

"Am I undead?" she asked, and knew it was a dumb-Dora question because she could feel her heart racing with excitement and arousal. According to good old Bram Stoker, the living dead didn't have heartbeats.

"Not undead. Very much alive, but changed. Immortal, though not unkillable. Vampire."

"Nifty!" She planned to enjoy every second of that eternal life, knowing Harry would share her joy. She could feel him again now, distant, but no more than he had been in Europe, or even when they'd been at separate colleges. "Can I change into a bat?"

"Only in silly books. And there are rules. You are a creature of the night now, of darkness…"

Lily was on her feet, fastening Johann's tuxedo jacket over her bare skin. "Piffle. Night's one thing—lots of swell stuff happens at night—but darkness? We have electricity these days."

He stared at her in bewilderment, then started to laugh. "Lily, I think I took away your pain too well. You will be a most unusual vampire."

"Just call me a vamp." Lily ran barefoot toward the garage. She knew this wild joint where no one would think twice about a girl wearing nothing but a tuxedo jacket. Might as well go cut the rug until the sun came up.

Johann shrugged and followed her.

FAIR PLAY

G. B. Kensington

She was a starveling thing, casually slurping congealed chicken lo mein from a takeout box she'd dug out of the dumpster at her back. He let her hear him coming, allowed his footsteps to echo off the buildings looming up into the night. As she watched him approach, he watched her try not to tense, to betray her sudden wariness.

Smiling, he pulled his hands from his overcoat's pockets and held them up to show that they were empty. "I come in peace."

She didn't smile. In fact, she grunted, her fingers tightening on her chopsticks. Odd, that. Usually, ladies licked their lips at his smile. Of course, she wasn't exactly a *lady*.

Strangely amused, he nodded at the box clenched in her other hand. "Care to trade up?"

The wariness in her expression hardened into outright suspicion. Oh, yes. This was truly a child of the streets, though she must be at least old enough to buy her own cigarettes. The hunger, never truly sated, turned over in his chest.

Deliberately, her narrowed eyes never leaving his face, she plucked a small white thing that probably wasn't a piece of rice out of her takeout box and flicked it aside. "You're dressed a little too fancy to be interested in my"—again deliberately, she jiggled the box—"leftovers."

He laughed, low and rich. His laugh was better than his voice, or so he'd been told. It seemed to work, anyway, as she relaxed enough to quirk a small grin. Ah, she *did* know the game, and it looked like she was finally ready to play.

"While lo mein *à la* dumpster is tempting, my girl, I think you'd like something a bit more…fresh. I happen to have ordered the most exquisite dinner on my way home tonight, only to remember that I'd be dining alone."

The grin turned to a smirk, and he could almost see her internal works switch from *watch out* to *haggle*. "What's on the menu?"

"Filet mignon, roasted potatoes, fresh-baked bread, a light salad, and all the wine you can drink."

Her narrow face tilted to one side, eyes narrowing again. "And sex?"

He huffed a soft chuckle, careful to keep his teeth hidden, for now. "After the raspberry cheesecake."

"Do you have a name?"

"Do you?"

She smiled, and the genuine expression lit up her whole face, shining through the grunge of her life on the streets, and for a moment, she was stunningly beautiful. This time, it wasn't his hunger turning over but something much lower. He half turned toward the safely lighted street at the end of the alley and lifted his cocked elbow.

"Shall we?"

Tossing away the takeout box, she sashayed over to him and took the offered elbow with one nail-bitten, grimy hand.

* * *

Her name was Adella, and she came out of her hour-long bath looking—and smelling—like a different person. The silken robe he'd given her outlined how pitifully thin she was, but free of the grime and grit of weeks without running water, her hair was a thick, glossy black. Her cheeks had blushed cherry red from the heat of her bath, but the color only pointed up how pale the rest of her was.

And her eyes...

"Better?"

She smiled, her eyes twinkling like the emeralds they resembled. From behind her filthy bangs in the harsh but distant glow of the streetlights, those eyes had looked a vague, dull gray. It was amazing how much difference candlelight and the prospect of a fabulous meal made.

"Much. You got a lot of soap for a guy. Swing both ways?"

He surprised himself by feeling insulted by the question. Only her casual sincerity kept him from lashing out at her. That, and his hasty mental reminder that this generation didn't see such pastimes as the abominations his own had. Even a few centuries didn't blunt that knee-jerk reaction to what would have been a death sentence in his own day.

He cleared his throat and attempted his *charming* smile. "Call me metrosexual, if you will. I have only one preference in my bed." The smile twisted a bit. "And it doesn't have the same equipment that I do."

She snorted, then tilted her face again, her expression suddenly serious. Was she studying him? And what did she see? A lonely but handsome businessman with more money than ability to keep a woman, or a predator on the prowl? Did she notice the sharper eyeteeth or the manicured cleanliness of his fingernails? The slowly building hunger making his eyes a brighter, more electric blue or the fashionable cut of his Italian suit?

"You said something about filet mignon?"

Both relieved and chagrined, he gestured toward the laden table and smiled when her stomach let out a painful-sounding growl. She didn't stand on ceremony. A slice of bread was in her hand and halfway down her throat before she'd fully settled in her chair, and she was too involved in her meal to notice that he only cut his meat into pieces instead of eating any of it, that his potatoes were merely pushed from one side of his plate to the other, that he didn't bother with the salad at all. He did sip a glass of wine, but only the one. It never settled well, though it was sometimes nice to be able to ingest something besides the one thing for which he always hungered.

She ate, and she ate well. In fact, he wondered if she would simply fall asleep as soon as she put down her fork or perhaps throw up the rich bounty her stomach couldn't be used to.

She did neither. Instead, she patted her lips with a cloth napkin, gulped down another half-glass of wine, and then sat back in her chair to stare fixedly at him. Had she noticed that he didn't actually eat anything before him? Would it matter? He had fed her, after all. Would she balk at feeding him in return?

But again, she surprised him. "You still haven't told me your name."

So fixated on only the now: was this what a lifetime of eating out of dumpsters had bought her? No care for what was or what would be, but absolute focus on what was directly in front of her? Was that survivalism or a dangerous blindness?

"I'm called James by most."

"By most, huh?" She tilted her face again, like a curious dog. "What does your mother call you? Jimmy?"

Smiling faintly, he shook his head.

"Jim? Jimbo? Jimmy Crack Corn?"

He chuffed a laugh through his nose and fiddled with his wineglass. "Enough. My name is Jameson Everleigh. Those few who know me well call me James."

"Sounds British."

Again, he smiled faintly. "Does it?"

"Tell me, James," she said with a crooked grin. "do you often dig helpless waifs out of the trash to wine and dine and spank their behind?"

He raised one eyebrow. "Are you always so direct?"

Shrugging, she touched her fingertips to the knot holding her robe in place. "I just want to know what I'm in for. You're beautiful, and you probably know it, but that doesn't mean you aren't a sicko."

Hunger twisted inside him at the nervousness betrayed by both gesture and word. So many dark impulses boiled inside him. Blood, he could live with, especially when it was sweetened with sex. But blood and *fear*, blood and *pain*...oh, the *salt* in that depthless sweet....

Swallowing hard, he forced his eyes to meet hers, and, for the first time since she'd taken his arm in the alley, he saw a flicker of the native wariness there. His eyes must be glowing with the hunger by now, and he tried to force it down.

"No fear, my lovely Adella. I only offer fair coin. Equal return for my investment." His mouth twisted in something that wasn't quite a smile. "Pain is not part of the equation."

The wariness didn't leave those gleaming green eyes, but it didn't worsen, either. "What are you, a stockbroker?"

"Sometimes."

She hesitated a long moment, and he wondered if he had made a mistake; if she was, for perhaps the first time in her life, studying the Big Picture. Putting all the pieces together.

Frowning, she tugged at her robe's belt. "Do I need to know?"

Everything inside him stilled in anticipation. "No."

Would she see that unnatural stillness, the frigid focus of the predator waiting to strike? Did she feel the tension drawing the air between them like a strained violin string?

She nodded slowly and stood. "Then let's go."

The string snapped, and he pounced.

Her naked body was woefully thin. Unfortunately, she would never be a supermodel. The layer of tough, ropy muscle covering her delicate skeletal structure made her unsuitable for the skin-and-bones look of most cover girls. Though her breasts were small, her hips narrow, and the crests of her pelvic bone jutted sharply, her ghostly white skin was marred here and there by the ragged scars of a lifetime of fighting for food and clothing and shelter.

No, she looked more like the gritty survivor of some global apocalypse—a superplague perhaps, or a zombie infestation—than one of the Beautiful People. In fact, she reminded him of a painting he once saw of a woman so grotesquely thin and twisted that she was starkly, ethereally beautiful; breathtaking, even.

Like that painting, his lovely Adella possessed an elemental appeal: her narrow, watchful face; those incredible eyes; the fragile strength of her survivalist frame glimpsed for the slightest moment before he tasted her mouth.

"Adella." He breathed her name, and she pressed against him with a throaty moan. "Adella, I need you. *Now.*"

She reached down and cupped the bulge of his swelling cock through his tailored slacks. It twitched and hardened further, and he groaned. His head fell back as she gave him a not-too-gentle stroke.

"I'm underdressed, James."

The hunger knifed through his chest, and he stripped so quickly she squawked to find him suddenly naked against her. The warming satin of her skin only stoked his cold, vicious need higher, and he didn't wait to lay her down on the bed. On the edge of control, he lifted her off the floor and shoved his aching, straining cock inside her.

She cried out, and part of him remembered that he'd promised her no pain, but most of him was already gone. She was tight on the inside and taut on the outside, her body already slickening for him as he thrust, his fingers digging into the tough muscle of her ass to move her as he wished. Grunting as he fucked her, he braced his feet apart and relied on his centuries-honed balance to keep him upright as he tried to balk the desperate hunger inside him enough to mask the pain of his initial invasion with building ecstasy.

She clung to him with all of the wiry strength in her body, wrapping her legs around his waist and seeking his mouth with her own. He avoided too wild a kiss, though. If his teeth nicked her tongue with this much raw need riding him, he'd skip right to feeding and break his promise. He would have his blood, yes, but not at the expense of her pleasure or his honor.

Pounding into her, he felt his grip on that resolve slip, felt the hunger gnaw at him, trying to tear itself out of him and into her, and he cried out at the mix of agony and nirvana warring inside him. It was always like this. Sometimes he broke, and the beast he tried so hard to hide would have its blood salted by the flood of fear and pain it caused.

This time, he refused, thrusting harder, even as her cries inched up in register until they were almost screams, even as her ragged nails dug at his back. He hammered that tight, clutching heat, drunk-walking the line between fucking hard and unleashing his full, devastating strength.

She came with a wrenching shudder and a harsh utterance too low-pitched to be a scream but too forceful for a moan, and he gratefully followed after, though he was far from done. The worst, biting edge of hunger flowed out of him with his semen, and he leaned his forehead on her heaving, sweaty chest, panting more from the effort of holding back than from exertion.

"James...*god*..."

He murmured nothings against her heated skin, forcing the lingering dregs of his need to the back corners of his mind. When he could think, he walked to the bed and laid them both down, her thin little body lost under his tall, muscled frame, her legs still clenched around him as if she feared he would pull out and leave her alone.

"My lovely Adella."

His voice was whiskey-rough, and she shivered wordlessly.

"Are you hurt, lovely one? I should have prepared you, but you stole my resolve."

Instead of answering, she fisted a hand in his hair and pulled his head back, stared up at him with those gleaming eyes, and then kissed him hard, her teeth pressing at his lips until he opened them for her tongue. A shudder wrenched through him, his cock sliding inside her moist heat, and he let her fuck him that way, thrusting her tongue toward his throat, her mouth feeding against his, her teeth bloodying her own lips as they ground against his.

That taste...god above, the sweet nectar of her very essence offered so freely...if he hadn't already sated the worst edge of the hunger....

His hands cupped her jaws and chin, holding her still as he pulled away to suckle at the tempting flow. It would be so easy to sink in his teeth, to rend that fragile skin, to bathe his face in the spray when he tore open her throat.

He swelled inside her at the thought, and she moaned long and loud when he slowly withdrew, then just as slowly pressed back inside. Using the very edge of his strength, he shoved the head of his cock hard against her womb, and she jolted against him, gasping and throwing her head back.

The move sliced her lower lip against one of his eyeteeth, and he stared helplessly at the trickle of fresh blood as it followed the curve of her lip to the corner of her mouth, puddled there, then rolled over her cheek and into her hair. Amazing how her own teeth grinding against that same lip had barely produced a hint of blood, but the merest nick from his had loosed this small flood.

His teeth...his *fangs*...

The hunger rose up again, but less fiercely this time. This hunger he could use; he would drive her over the edge of purest euphoria before he assuaged it.

Another shove of his hips, his cock not bumping but *pounding* against her womb, and she arched beneath him, crying out to the ceiling. He set a steady pace, not fucking this time but not making love, either, until she writhed beneath him, sobbing his name. He lowered his face to her chest and kissed her tiny breasts, so tempted to sink in his teeth, his *fangs*, to taste of her and fill himself with her even as he filled her, to feed on her as she had been fed.

His lovely Adella. A delicate, wayward lamb led so trustingly to slaughter.

No!

That was the beast's voice. He jerked his head back as his teeth grazed her skin, two beads of blood welling where his fangs had touched. Not yet. He wouldn't feed yet, and he wouldn't feed to his fullest.

Not this time.

As if in rebellion against this resolve, the hunger twisted anew inside him, the scent of spilled blood driving it to its painful edge. He growled and jerked to his knees, buried to the hilt in the hot, sucking beauty of her tiny body, and thrust with more force than he'd dared to use in years. Her back arched up off the bed, her breath leaving her on a rush of wind without vocalization. Again—and she dug her fists into the sheets. Again—and his cock pulsed in time with the agonized throbbing of his starving heart. Again—and she came apart for the second time, that gloriously chiseled body clutching him inside and out, guttural noises escaping her locked-up throat as her lungs strained for air that wouldn't come.

And he laughed, not because he wanted her to choke on the pleasure he'd thrust upon her but because the hunger, the beast he could never fully chain, rose up inside him and made him thrust again while she suffered her release, and she came again, or just kept coming, her face reddening as she tried to breathe through the excruciating ecstasy.

And *now* he struck, blanketing her with his infinitely stronger body as his fangs sank into the vulnerable line of her straining throat. The monstrous beast that was his body kept thrusting, kept stabbing his stupid, throbbing, senseless cock into her while he drank from the fount of her life, sucking her down as her body sucked him in, filling him up, filling all the empty places, bringing him fully to life.

But before that gushing, hot flood slowed, he tore himself away, wrestling the beast back into its reluctant cage even as he licked at the luscious spill of blood on his lips and chin. The beast wouldn't have her. Not his lovely Adella. The hunger wouldn't win this time, no matter how good it was to feel her life raging through him as if it were his own.

When he was sure it was safe, he looked down at her,

at the steady pulse throbbing in her neck, at the already-scabbing wound there that would heal before morning. Somewhere between her climax and his feeding, she had finally remembered how to breathe, but she was out cold, either asleep or actually unconscious. Her heavy lashes fanned her cheeks, the dark patches under her eyes making her look more hollowed out than before. Exhausted, likely, and missing a pint or two of blood, but she would live.

And she would never know how she had truly paid for her fine meal and hot bath. He would swear to that.

Slowly, savoring her taste, he licked away the last dregs of blood from her throat, cleaning the skin as thoroughly as she must have done herself earlier. When even the tiniest hint was gone, he simply lay against her, holding her body close and remembering how it felt to be alive, to be warm and wide awake, to lie against a lover instead of a stranger, to be...to not be a monster.

Smiling against the crook of his lovely Adella's neck, he fell asleep.

He had fed well. Thus, he had slept well. Had slept the clock around, in fact.

Adella was gone. The bed was cold and, for some reason, his pillow was missing its case. Shrugging, he all but leapt from the bed, feeling more alive than he had for many moons.

He hadn't allowed himself to feed so fully for at least a decade, fearing yet another bloody mess to clean up, another body to hide. It felt good to be so wide awake. Colors fairly blazed at him from all corners of his bedroom, even in the dark.

Grinning and feeling like a new man, he stretched to his fullest, yawned hugely, then paused and tilted his head to one side, much like Adella had done so many times. The wall across from his bed was bare. The Monet that had hung there since the end of the Second World War was gone. The wallpaper, a deep red everywhere else, was as dark as blood in the space where it had hung.

Frowning, he stalked over and touched that darker section of wall, trying to get his wide-awake brain to supply him with a reason for this oddity. After all, the nail was still in place. Only the painting and its expensive frame were gone.

Eyes narrow, he slowly turned around, now picking out the familiar furnishings that he barely even noticed under usual circumstances. His etched silver letter opener was gone, as was its silver tray. The heavy silver candlesticks had left behind their candles. A small gilt mirror, gone. And his pillowcase.

Surely, she wouldn't have...

A scowl settled into his forehead, and he flashed over to his dresser and the closed jewelry box there. He'd collected two centuries' worth of rings and tiepins and cufflinks and heavy necklace chains. His hand hesitated as his fingers touched the age-darkened wood of a jewelry box that had traveled here with him from Europe a century before, and his scowl darkened.

He opened the box. The first tray was empty. Closing his eyes, he lifted out the first tray and felt in the second. His fingertips touched only crushed velvet.

She'd taken it all.

Opening his eyes, he forced himself to walk out of his bedroom, down the hall, and into the living room to his coat by the door. He drew out his wallet and knew before he even opened it that the cash inside was missing. Probably a thousand dollars, gone.

His credit cards were all in place, though, as was his license and other identifying information. A clever thief, then. She hadn't taken anything that would lead him to her if she used it. Oh, he could likely track down certain pieces of the jewelry when she pawned it off, but she would certainly be gone long before he could arrive. Nowadays, he'd find her far more quickly for using his credit cards than pawning his brother's old pocket watch. Hell, the credit house would probably find her for him.

What she didn't know was that, now that he'd tasted her, he could find her anywhere in the world. She would never be safe again. She could never hide from him.

Unless…

Unless he *let* her.

Some emotion bubbled up inside him, and when he opened his mouth to express it, he had no idea what to expect. Thus, the deep, echoing belly laughs caught him a bit off guard. The surprise didn't stop his laughter, though, and he stood naked in his living room, howling up at the ceiling like a lunatic and wondering how many men she'd conned, his lovely Adella.

His amusement cycled down, and he stuffed his wallet back into his coat. The cash was easily replaced, after all. He wouldn't track her down.

She had more than earned the trinkets she'd taken with her as he slept, coasting on the blood high she'd given him. Even his favorite Monet was a small price to pay for the energy welling up inside him, for the warmth pulsing through his veins, for the colors all but bursting from the walls. She could have his things as fair trade for what he'd taken from her, even if she never knew.

After all, it was a brand-new night, and he felt like a ripe youth again. Smiling with the simple pleasure of living, he nodded once and headed for the bathroom and a nice, hot bath. He intended to enjoy it to its fullest.

And, if he knew his Adella, somewhere, she was doing the same.

ADVANTAGE

Ciara Finn

Think of it," says Jude, his body against my back, "as an evolutionary advantage. We are predators, after all."

The Snake Pit is a low square room in the basement below a condemned apartment block; it's thick with smoke and music, voices and lust. It's not a club you can find a flyer for; you have to be a Pit native to get asked in. You meet new ones, every so often; the ones who want more risk, something more real; the ones who belong here, like me.

Predators; it's easy to forget. Jude's polished manners and the faint musk surrounding me are like something from Europe, something old. That musk is already working its hypnotic magic, it seems. But the hands that hold my hips are iron hard, and I know I couldn't get away if I tried. It's just as well I'm not interested in doing so. I keep my eyes on the tall one across the room; his shirt is open to the waist, and all over his narrow, muscled chest are silver sparkles. Body glitter, just like the emo kids in the city clubs. It's working; there's a woman talking to him. She looks like one of the ones who won't come here twice; though whether she'll scare herself or end up dead is another matter. I don't know the one with the glitter on; wouldn't know whether to risk my neck.

"I can't help thinking it's cheap."

Jude laughs, cool against my cheek. "I never said it wasn't."

"What's your advantage, then?"

Jude turns me, and I'm looking into eyes that are a little too amber to be brown.

"Your weakness for vampires," he says. His lips are cold when he kisses me, like his breath, and gooseflesh stirs on my skin; the only warmth Jude has is what I give him. All around me is that musk, thick and dark, earthy as the grave; it's their lure, their venom, the thing that fogs your mind and lets them close in. No vampire looks even remotely human, close up; too pale, too hard, too still. Too beautiful. Jude's chestnut hair is neatly tied, his lips no redder than mine now I've been kissed, but the chill of him is striking into my skin. I can't help but shiver, and it's not entirely with cold.

"A weakness for predators," I say. "I'm going to get myself killed."

"Someday." He goes to kiss my neck; I tense. He smiles and pulls back, cat-and-mouse. "Don't you trust me, Alice?"

"With my life." Literally.

"I think it's time to leave."

I don't get to argue, not with this. I'm not sure I could; I'm hazy with drink and the opium of Jude's presence. I see streets passing me by, Jude's arm like a railing at my back. Then a door, a staircase; Jude's immense bed, dark wooden posts and plum-colored sheets. A cold fingertip strokes my neck, ghosts down to the curve of my breast; my nipples tighten. I reach for Jude's shirt. The room around us is dark as a cave, night-colored walls and a thick carpet that muffles sound; but he seems to pull the light in, to stand in a place of his own. His chest is smooth; as I push the shirt from his shoulder the shadows leave it, and it's white as all his skin. I curl my hand around his shoulder blade, dig my nails in; he bares his teeth a little, in a smile. I can already see the tips of his fangs. I rake my nails down the plane of his chest; they leave no marks, just faint indentations in the skin that disappear. If he was a man, he'd be breathing hard, but his rib cage is still.

He moves like ice sliding on a sheet of glass. His hands close on my waist, push under the poor excuse for a top; my breath catches. Jude likes to take his time; he undresses me slowly, lifting away cheap cotton, stroking chill, possessive hands over my shoulders, slipping the fine, black straps of my bra down and freeing my breasts. That cold mouth on my nipples is a shock that makes me gasp. His teeth scrape, he makes a low, snarling sound.

He's hungry. I'm going to get bitten tonight.

"Oh god," I say quietly, on a rush of arousal. Jude's eyes flash up to mine.

"You're not going to fight me, Alice," he says. "You're not that stupid, not after all this time."

"So tie me down."

Jude's hands pin my wrists at my sides. I want to struggle, but I want to live. Fighting them's a bad idea; it enrages them. They lose control; a lot like men. But provoking a man gets you rough sex, if you're lucky; provoking a vampire is a good way to die. I don't struggle, but I'm tense as a bow. Jude pushes me back toward the bed, bears me down with his weight and spreads my arms. He's warming; my body heat seeping into him. The hard whiteness of his chest against mine is no longer cold as marble, merely cool. I hear the snap of steel cuffs locking into place around my wrists; thick padding makes them bearable.

"Now," Jude says, as I shift and pull against the ropes. Prone like this, heat must be rising off me like smoke from incense; he leans down to draw in long breaths, tasting the warmth of my neck and the scent of my skin. He licks the warmest spots, making me shiver; the hollow of my neck, my arms. He rolls his hips against me, and I feel him, hard. It tells me I'm wet already too, the way my cheap lace knickers slide against my skin.

"Jude," I say. "I want you. Fuck me."

His eyes meet mine and they look brighter, harder. He's halfway there; halfway to losing what remains of Jude the man. His hands go to my belt, unfasten my jeans by touch alone. As he pulls them down, cool air hits my skin, and he snarls again and buries his face in the opening. Heat, heat and the smell of human skin; it draws them like nothing else. The hottest place on my body is my slick and swollen cunt, and Jude rips my jeans off, tears the knickers as he pulls them away. That's why I buy them cheap; they don't last long. I'm naked, exposed to him now, tied to the bed and laid out for the predator to take; but Jude pulls back. He looks me over, runs a slow hand up my thigh. I go with Jude because he's like a cat; he plays with his food. His tongue, almost warm to my skin, traces lines up my legs that make me arch my back. I'm aching, my clit hard and wanting to be touched, and he won't go near me, won't let himself have my warmth until he's ready to take it. He's biting now, little warning nips along my belly, and I can feel his fangs; they're lengthening.

"Jude. Please."

He laughs, and one long finger slides inside me. I gasp and arch my back. It's not enough. I try to work myself on it, and he takes it away.

"Bastard!"

His teeth close hard on the fleshy mound above my clit, and I go as still as I can. I heard about a girl who said the wrong thing, and the scars she had. There is a moment of pure panic in me, I lie there frozen. Slowly, he releases me, and that's when I feel his cool, pointed tongue. He doesn't care about my pleasure; it's a side effect. All he wants is warmth, the taste of me. If it feels good, he gets more of that. Enough to make him want me; enough to bite. Sometimes, they'll lose it and go for the artery in your thigh; messy, and it's a pretty sure kill. They rip you apart to get to it. I've never heard of Jude doing that to anyone.

Yet.

His fingers slide into me again. I groan with pleasure, tightening around them; I've never been able to help the way danger turns me on. Jude's breathing now, drinking in my scent; he sounds almost human, like a man.

"Jude, Christ. I want your cock. Fuck me, Jude, I'm hot, can't you feel how hot I am?"

Jude stops moving, and lifts himself on one hand. His eyes are lambent and his fangs are out, long and vanishing to nothing at all at the point.

"Yes," he says, a hiss through the space they leave. "Yes I can."

He takes his time even now, slowly unfastening his belt; slowly freeing himself. His cock is a column of porcelain, his body white stone; his balance is impossible as he strips right there on the bed. As he comes down over me I can't help but pull against the restraints; he's only warm where he's been touching me, and that's not much. I shudder, and he holds me down by my waist, and slides himself in.

Some of them are rough and fast; Jude's so slow it's sadistic. He tortures me because he's doing it to himself, delaying his pleasure to get a bigger hit. He moves like glass, smooth and powerful, and his cock's like ice sliding into my cunt, cold as hell and I can't help but arch. I grind against him with every stroke; he pulls back, almost to the tip of his cock, and I feel it heating up, a blunt warmth where my cunt's cold from him. Vampires are hard all over, no human give, and his cock is too; fucking him is like the best kind of beating: punishing, and so good. I wrap my thighs around him, drawing him deeper in; where he's inside me he's warm, but his back is cold, cold as a snake's skin.

He bends his head to the hollow of my neck; breathes me in again. For a moment I think *this is it*, then he throws back his head with a groan and his rhythm speeds up. God, he likes it, teasing himself—but he's grinding down on me hard and I was already close, under his tongue. I'm going to come, from that unyielding cock shoving tight in again and again; it's the way it catches my G-spot, doesn't bend. I let myself moan and lock my ankles behind his back; Jude *growls*, and that's when I see him give in.

Under all of them there's an animal—men, vampires, either one. Jude's orange-yellow eyes, the red lips that pull back over those vicious fangs, they're the truth of him; and that truth drives into me, lands me hard in my body, pierced by a hot shaft. Jude's sucked my own heat in and now it's fucking me in return. I feel my cunt squeezing him, tighter and tighter; he's gripping me by my shoulder and my neck, his back starting to arch as he gets closer to the bite. He tenses, and at the top of his stroke he presses up, pushing my G-spot, hitting my cervix just right, and I cry out; Jude thrusts one more time, his head rolls back, and I come as he snaps down, and sinks in his fangs.

I scream raggedly, shaking on his cock and held totally still, the blood that flushes me draining into him. I can't breathe, hypersensitive to the pressure of his lips, but whether it's from coming or the blood loss I can't say. Maybe I black out; I come to when Jude pulls off me, almost as if he's coming himself. He looks down at me, a naked moment of unity between us. I feel weak, my heart pounding as it tries to sustain me with what little it has left. Jude slashes his thumb as his fangs begin to retract, and swipes it over the wounds on my neck; they sting hard as they heal over.

"You took...a lot—"

"You're not going to die."

No I'm not, but I sure as hell can't move. Jude seems to realize that, and swears softly under his breath. The world blackens around the edges, and I pass out again.

I wake the next morning wrapped in a blanket, on a couch in the back room of the Snake Pit. This happens sometimes. Today, I'm the only one. My clothes are folded neatly on a chair, and I feel a hell of a lot less bad; when I free my arm and look at it, I see a cannula mark. Someone gave me blood. I should find out who it was.

I dress, and leave the place; the door's not locked. Nobody in his right mind would try robbing them. No one ever tries it twice, anyway. Outside the sun is bright; I'm still light-headed. I'll be needing a good steak dinner, but I'm okay. It feels good, so good, to be alive.

In the sharp shadows of an alleyway, something stirs. I pause by the entrance.

"Till next time, Jude," I say.

I hear something between a snarl and a laugh. They're careful, the clever ones, always careful never to leave a mess. Never shit where you eat, that's what they say. I'm clever too; but as I walk on, the sun streaming onto my sweating, human back, I know I won't always win. Someday I won't be clever enough; someday I'll die from this. Someday one of them will be too hungry, too fast. Or I'll be in the wrong mood, I'll run my mouth that inch too far, and push Jude over the edge.

Or I'll let myself believe you can trust them the way you'd trust a man, to feel for you. I feel that tug with Jude sometimes; even now I want his eyes to be following me, hungrily. But I don't care about it now. I don't go to the Snake Pit for thrills or for status. I don't even go for the sex. I go because of this: as I walk away from Judas, from the shadows into the light, I feel almost innocent again.

THE COMMUNION OF BLOOD AND SEMEN

Maxim Jakubowski

On a day like this I held her tight.

On a day like this, she put her head on my shoulder, said nothing but almost purred. It felt good. It felt right. She was wrapped up in layers of clothing like in a cocoon as she sheltered herself from the daylight on this day like no other. My gift-wrapped impossible fuck.

The sky was blue, not a cloud in sight and a chilly wind channeled its way down the city streets, insidiously digging its way through the fabric of our coats, freezing the bones all the way under the skin.

Her hands reached for mine.

"Your skin is so warm," she said.

Hers was as cold as ice.

Had always been.

Her eyes were shielded from the brightness by dark glasses. I'd never known her without the glasses, even at night. Maybe that's what first actually caught my attention about her. I'd always felt that people who wear shades in all and inappropriate circumstances were pretentious, poseurs or worse. She'd been the exception.

A yellow cab drew up on McDougall, responding to my arm signal.

"JFK," I said as we bundled into the car. We had no luggage.

We'd met in Manhattan. On, of all places, Craigslist, the Internet Sargasso of obscene desire, barter, thievery, fakery and false identities. I was traveling on business and feeling lonely, as endless New York nights stretched on forever as both jet lag and the repeated assault of bittersweet memories combined fiendishly to keep me awake most of the night with my hand not far from my cock, caressing myself aimlessly as I recalled the walk down from Washington Square to Ground Zero with Gina, and the rubber stamp embossed with the words *I Love You* I'd bought along the way at a gift shop on Broadway, tendrils of lust rising through the thick trunk of my awakening cock. Remembering a night at the Gershwin Hotel where, in a spirit of mad improvisation, I'd crushed a few raspberries and pushed the pulp inward with two fingers up the cunt of the New Zealand woman I'd picked up a few days before at Newark airport, and then followed the fragrant fruit with a square of chocolate that quickly melted in the furnace of her innards before I finally lapped it all up with my tongue before we fucked: my cock now becoming half hard and just that bit longer and sending a hundred volts of sexual electricity all the way through my groin. The apartment a few blocks up from Columbus Circle where I'd mounted Pamela, the wife of an experimental Armenian jazz musician, and breached her sphincter quite roughly as Bruce Springsteen's "Candy's Room" from the *Darkness on the Edge of Town* album punctuated our rhythmic thrusts on the record player: by this memory I was hard again, at last. But there was no point evoking other New York memories, of women, of bodies, of heartbreak: jerking myself off at three in the morning in a hotel bed would, I knew all too well, bring me no relief. It would not banish the thoughts, the images, the faces, the cunts (every single one so different, so unique I could lose myself in a whole novel of genital descriptions, a journey through craters, gashes, crevices and infinite deeps of soft, ridged alluring flesh....) I needed reality, a body, eyes looking into mine as I caressed her skin, the smell of tobacco or food on her breath, the fragrance of a woman's sweat, the beating of a heart deep inside.

So, I'd placed an ad online under Casual Encounters: *Visiting English Writer Seeks Companionship and Tenderness.* Within a few hours there were three responses: Sarah just wanted to exchange emails about books but was reluctant to meet; Becky, who worked in a museum in Brooklyn, joined me for sushi in Greenwich Village the next day but was too young and thick-waisted and just kept on talking about her college boyfriend; and Carmilla. Of course, I'd read Le Fanu and the name and its vampiric allegiance appealed. There was a sense of danger about her. *I am available,* she said, and the smile on her jpeg spoke of sensuality and a curious sense of destiny. *If you enjoy taking risks.*

I'd not enjoy life if there were no risks to face. Risk brings you alive, I replied in my email.

Little did I know.

We met.

She was even better than in the photo.

Her eyes like pools of black soot.

It was night. A small bar near Bleecker Street.

Within minutes I knew I had to have her.

I was surprised by the dry coldness of her flesh when I soon undressed her—we had wasted little time on preliminaries or undue conversation; somehow an exchange of meaningful glances, signals and silences had been enough to confirm that the No Strings Attached encounter we had both been seeking was going to happen there and then that same night. But she sheltered quickly within my embrace and my external warmth migrated over across the maddeningly smooth landscape of her flesh and spread its comforting currents. The scarlet lipstick that illuminated her features soon stained my lips and my own skin. Her small, hard breasts with night-dark nipples sharp as blunt razors were grazing my chest, and even with the hotel room's main light off the delta of her cunt was like a beacon in the heart of the darkness that surrounded us. We fucked. As soon as I was inside of her, I knew this was where I had always aspired to live, sheathed within her tightness, sliding effortlessly against the ribbed texture of her damp walls. Our mouths savagely vacuumed the contents of the other's lungs in unholy communion. I came quickly. Exhaled. But her cunt still gripped my cock like a vise and would not allow it to go soft. She arched her back under me.

"Do me again?" she asked me.

I shifted, the tip of my penis now moving against her cervix. The coldness inside her drew me in even farther. Her nails scratched my back and the pain felt good. It all felt good.

It was primitive, no doubt the way our ancestors first mated in deep forests under a pockmarked moon. It was right. It made us both feel so abominably alive.

Later, she took me inside her mouth, licking the primordial soup we had jointly created, which I had already tasted with relish after I'd gone down on her and savored our combined and now intermingled fluids and secretions. As I expected, we were a totally perfect cocktail even if, at first, my tongue delving

into her had initially drawn back from the unaccustomed cool-
ness of her insides, even after the repeated and frantic sex we
had enjoyed. Her own tongue was at first as cold as ice but that
only served to conserve my hardness. She licked and nibbled,
allowing her teeth to teasingly draw sharp, hard lines against my
aching, bulbous and purple head.

"I want to bite you," she remarked, her voice flat, neither in
jest nor in lust.

"Somehow, I don't think I'd even mind," I responded with
a smile.

I was hoping my joke would make her laugh, but instead
when I looked down at her face there between my thighs, her red
lips still voraciously sucking on my cock, I noticed a single tear
running down her cheek.

I chose not to comment.

Finally, we exhausted ourselves. We were both raw, aching in
all the right places, coated with a patina of sweat and god knows
what else and we must have fallen asleep simultaneously.

When I woke up some hours later, it must have been daylight
outside, but the curtains were drawn. She was sitting on the
opposite edge of the bed, with her back to me. The shape of
her naked body was like a knife stabbing my heart: she was so
fucking beautiful, every pale curve silhouetted against the muted
light trying to enter the room was like a symphony of harmony,
balance and grace. The fall of her dark straight hair against her
elegant shoulders, the shadow of her delicate breasts, the arch
of her vertebrae straining gently against the skin, the faint down
in the small of her back, the upper moon of her white ass; every
body part reminded me of other women I had known, loved, and
pined for: Gina's ass, Kathryn's breasts, Aida's hair…. But here
they all came together in perfect harmony. My heart skipped a
beat and my cock hardened yet again.

She heard me move and turned her face toward me. Her shoulders swiveled and I saw that her nipples were still as pointy and hard and aroused. She had put her dark glasses on again.

We ordered breakfast from room service. There was no way we were leaving that bed and I guessed anyone looking at us that morning would have read every visible sign of debauchery and excess all over the two of us like an open page. She only wanted fruit juice. I also had a bagel with salmon and cream cheese. I was famished from our exertions.

"Aren't you hungry?" I queried.

Her eyes looked down at the mess of the sheets in which we'd drowned our lust.

"No."

There was a finality in her tone.

Soon after, we pushed the breakfast tray onto the hotel room floor and she lowered her head toward my lap and again took my cock inside her mouth. The coldness and the fire returned, an uncanny duo of emotions and feelings.

Later I asked, "Have you met many other guys this way through the Internet?"

"A few... It's the only way I can satisfy that hunger inside, you see," she remarked matter-of-factly, in no way apologetic.

"I think I understand," I said.

And so the next few days went on, in a whirlpool of madness, flesh rubbing against flesh, mouths drowning in the thin air from which we'd sucked all the oxygen in our frenzy of desire, body parts inflamed, stretched obscenely. We drew the worst out of each other, as if never before had we even skirted those dark borders of absolute need. We had no shame, no limits. I fisted her, hurt her even, but she begged me to push harder, farther. She squatted over my spent body and urinated on me as I rubbed the cool ambrosia that stemmed from her innards all over my skin.

Had she asked, I would have drunk from her cunt lips.

I don't know when we crossed the frontier from which there is no going back. Possibly the day I was scheduled to fly back to Europe and blithely missed my flight.

The more we stayed together, tested the very limits of our bodies, the more we knew we could never part. We now inhabited another world.

She scratched me badly one morning. Not deliberately. It was in fact surprising that the inherent violence in our movements, our coupling, had not caused more damage before. Sprains, bruises, cuts. The blood welled over my shoulder blade. Her sad features turned somehow even paler than usual as she watched the solitary drops of blood she had summoned lazily slide down over my chest like dark pearls.

"I feel like licking you," she said quietly.

"I wouldn't mind," I remarked. "Maybe it's the right way to celebrate our unholy union...."

"No," she said. "I would want you even more if I did."

She dispatched me to the bathroom to clean up. But her eyes said something else.

Another morning, I cut myself shaving and again the look that spread across her features was an unsteady blend of hunger and utter despair.

She walked toward me with all the burdens of the world weighing down her steps. Stopped just an inch away from me. Watching the minute flecks of blood on my chin. Her mouth opened. Her eyes clouded.

Right then it all finally came together.

Her unnatural pallor.

The ambiguous clues she had unwittingly provided me with.

The ever-present dark glasses and nocturnal life.

The origins of her name.

Why I never saw her eating food.

I asked her.

And she told me her story.

The tale of a beautiful vampire adrift in the confused life of a world in which she could never truly belong. How she survived.

How sex could sometimes act as a substitute for the blood-lust that kept her alive. But was never enough.

I'd read the innumerable books; heard the countless legends.

"And if I allowed you to taste my blood, bite me...what would happen?" I asked her.

"You know," she said.

Yes I knew. I would die, but awaken anew as a monster. Another freak who could only survive the madness by feeding on the blood of others. As she had done for centuries.

But I loved her now. Of that I had no doubt. And I wanted us to stay together. Forever.

Now we had met, now we had become as one, neither of us could ever bear the loneliness of being apart again.

"I will," I said.

I maxed my credit cards and we took a flight to Venice. Our hotel is a converted palazzo and from our windows we have a half-glimpse of the Grand Canal and farther upstream the still-ness of the lagoon. Maybe I'm too much of a romantic, but I wanted it to happen in a place like this.

On a day like this I have asked her to kill me so I can live forever and roam the land of death with her until the end of time, both now renegades, lovers in the blood, vampires.

NIGHTLIFE

Madeleine Oh

He caught my eye at once. I'd returned to Paris after a hiatus of seventy years or more, and on the third night, I found him in a nameless club among the tangled streets of the *Butte*. He was alone in the crowd; no doubt his air of despondency kept the surrounding roisterers at bay. Halfway to drunkenness, he seemed caught in the enveloping presence of humanity and the aroma of cheap wine.

I watched as he called for another carafe, which he drank alone. Perfect. I prefer the ones without companions—there's no one to remember me. This one was ideal: a morose expression on his bearded face, alcohol-drenched eyes and those absurd little lenses mortals use in their vain attempt to see as well as we do.

I sat down in the lone chair beside him.

"Go away," he said.

I laughed. (Who gives orders to a vampire?) And I met his eyes. He didn't quail or shudder as so many would, too far gone in his cups for that, but behind the dullness, I glimpsed a wild and wayward passion, a yearning for excitement and deep traces of suppressed longing.

I smiled carefully. It was too early to show my fangs. I touched his arm. "Come with me."

He rose and I understood the reason for his loneliness. He was a dwarf with the torso of a man. He looked at me, eyes bright with defiance and the expectation of rejection, as his wide mouth twisted in a warped smile. "Madame, you wish for my company tonight?"

I didn't waste words replying. Hadn't I made that abundantly clear, even to a half-drunken mortal? "Come," I repeated, keeping hold of his arm. "I offer a sweeter oblivion than cheap Algerian wine."

He laughed at that: a deep peal of mirth rooted in pain and awareness of the farce of mortal life. "Not a patch on the wines of Galliac, I agree, but it serves its purpose."

"I offer better."

We were in the street now. He tightened his coat against a gust of wind and looked at me. "Don't you feel the cold?"

Maybe a satin dress and a light stole were a little brief for January but I shook my head. "My kind do not feel heat or cold. Come."

He came. Few mortals can resist a vampire's call. We turned corners and crossed narrow streets. The scurrying rats and the stench of refuse belonged to the city of a hundred years ago. This was a Paris far removed from the wide, clean boulevards of Haussmann's new city. Not that the mortal noticed, too intent on the imagined pleasures ahead no doubt. But he did hesitate climbing the stairs to the rooms I'd acquired. Was it difficulty mounting the stairs on his attenuated legs? Or some inner sense that I was not the usual woman of the night?

He didn't hesitate long. Men: rich, poor, strong or crippled, all want the same from a woman. I give them that and take much more than they could ever imagine.

Once inside, he looked around my room, surprised perhaps that a woman he perceived to be of easy and available charms lived in such comfort. I did not choose to explain.

To forestall any conversation, I tossed my stole on a chair and removed my dress.

"Madame," he said, "you have a name as well as fine breasts?"

I walked over to him, to underscore my words and distract him from conversation. "I prefer sharing my breasts to sharing my name."

Curious and briefly alarmed, he asked, "I've never seen you before. Are you that known in this *quartier*?"

"Not at all. I have been out of Paris for many years." Before he or his father was born.

"Many?" he echoed, a wry smile on his wide mouth. "Not so many, I think, Madame. Unless you left in your nurse's arms."

Gallant in its way, I suppose, but I hadn't picked him for his charm. Why had I chosen him, the cripple, from a club peopled with healthy, upright men, any one of whom would gladly remove his trousers for me? What caught my eye? Apart from the briefly glimpsed passion behind his eyes, did I suspect a wild desire reined in behind his wall of pain and arrogance? Was I drawn to the quiet need traced on every line of his face? Perhaps it was simply a whim to stroke the rough darkness of his beard?

That was easily indulged in. I ran two fingers over the line of his jaw, tracing under his full lower lip and taking care not to pierce his skin with my nail. I wanted his blood—just not yet.

Knowing how much chill air diminished ardor and deflated

erections, I turned to add more wood to the stove. "The bed awaits you," I said.

He ignored my suggestion and crossed the room, taking the bundle of wood from my hands and adding to the stove. "You need a servant to do this."

"I have a servant." A girl I found in the streets and hired for more than a pimp would give her to prostitute herself. "She is abed. Should we not be?" I turned my back to him. "I would rather not wake her to undo my stays."

He did the honors, loosening the laces until I could ease my corset over my head. Even with that he assisted. Had I found a romantic? Or was he hesitant to disrobe and reveal his deformed legs?

All he had removed was his hat and gloves, placing then on a side table when he entered. It was time to see to the rest. I took his coat and hung that over the back of an upright chair.

"Sir," I said, "I think we both know why you accompanied me here."

He inclined his head with a quietly spoken, "But of course," as he removed his jacket and unbuttoned his waistcoat.

I chose to assist, running my hands over the woolen fabric and the fine linen of his shirt, inhaling the scents of laundry starch and male flesh disguised by cologne. His skin was mortal warm through the crisp fabric, mortal warm and awaiting me, as I unbuttoned his shirt and removed his silk cravat.

I let him cope with the stiff collar, contenting myself with watching as he discarded that and the shirt.

Then it was my turn. Mortal flesh never ceased to attract me and this man was no exception. His chest was warm and firm, the nipples dark and his hair soft and springy under my fingertips. I eased my hand down to the waist of his trousers, imagining the tighter curls clustered around his cock; assuming he wasn't as small there, as his legs.

I should have thought of that, but too late. If he was, I'd take his blood and leave him with fair memories. Why dally? I lowered my head and kissed him as I reached for the buttons at his waist.

His response distracted me. Wild passion and need burst from his lips like a tide of burning heat. Was it his desire or mine that flared between us as I pressed my lips to his and I pulled his head upward to anchor his mouth on mine?

He whimpered, moaned, as a sweet shudder rippled down his body and I reached my hand to cup his erection.

No lack of manliness there. He was hard and ready but I wanted far more from him than a fumbled fuck. I stepped back, aware of his racing heartbeat and heightened breathing and the glorious flush on his face that promised richness beneath his skin.

I said nothing in reply to his gasp but walked over to my bed, shedding chemise and petticoats on my way, and letting my pantaloons fall to the carpet. I stepped out of them, knowing full well he was watching. (What man with blood in his veins wouldn't?) To encourage him further I placed my foot on a nearby stool as I rolled down my stockings. Slowly. Without looking back, I climbed onto the bed and sat cross-legged, waiting.

I've seldom seen a man shed socks, shoes and trousers at such speed. He kept on his drawers. Modesty? I thought not. It would be pointless anyway.

I beckoned.

He didn't hesitate. Few mortals could.

We embraced again, a pleasant enough sensation by all measures—but it was his body, his blood, his jism that I hungered for and to take all I desired, I needed him secure. I broke the kiss. He lay in my arms, limp and pliant. Faster than a mortal could move I tied his hands to the headboard with silken cords.

His eyes widened with shock. He opened his mouth to protest so I brought mine down again. He did not, could not resist. Ignoring the restraints, he gave himself over to my lips and welcomed my tongue as I opened his mouth with mine.

That stifled any protests.

"There's nothing to fear," I told him as I stroked his chest and bent to lick his nipple. "I will not harm you," I went on, smiling at his hardening nipples.

"Then why restrain me, Madame?"

Ever polite, this one was. "To keep you in my bed," I replied and kissed his other nipple, nipping it gently to wring a groan from him. Much as the rhythm of his heartbeat tempted, I was not ready to draw blood. First pleasure, and then feed.

It seemed he accepted my word, or realized the futility of resistance. Perhaps he was one of those who enjoyed submission? No matter. I kissed his neck, stroked his chest, teased those proud nipples with my tongue and let him feel the caress of my fangs against his skin, all the while hiding them from his view.

Some of my kindred enjoy instilling fear and horror. I refrain, unless it is merited, as with the creature who abused my little servant. I enjoyed his cringing terror.

Seeing my man eager, his agitation having increased rather than diminished the bulge behind his drawers, I stroked his thighs, sensing the weakness beneath. What tragic fate had caused crippled legs on such a fine torso? I eased down his drawers and stared. In three hundred years I've seen many men, but never one this endowed.

It seemed nature, having cheated him on his legs, compensated him with this cock: stupendous in size, form and girth. Indeed, for a few moments, I wondered if I'd encountered a new form of mortal creature. It was as if his cock leeched strength and power from his legs and…

I was losing my concentration. I'd searched for a man to milk and found a colossus. Now I had to watch against gorging myself.

"You are indeed endowed by the gods."

"In one way only," he replied, his voice taut and harsh.

"The way that matters most to a woman," I replied and wondered about the spiteful mortal women who'd rejected him for his short stature when he possessed a prize beyond most lovers' dreams.

"You are fine indeed," I said, stroking my finger up the side of his cock until it twitched at me.

I licked my lips in anticipation and he laughed. "Madame, one would think you planned to make a meal of me."

"One would indeed," I replied, licking my lower lip as my fangs itched and pressed my gums. "I cannot but wonder how a man as endowed as you does not have a sweetheart or lover awaiting him. Why spend your evenings in the company of a bottle?"

Mistake. He growled at me. "A bottle makes an uncomplaining mistress."

More likely, a bottle offered oblivion, but his demons were not mine.

"I will not complain," I told him as I stroked his atrophied thighs. "I will devour you instead." And I closed my mouth over the head of his cock.

He gasped, but not from pain or shock. His hips jerked and I took him deeper. He groaned a few times as his spine arched and his frail legs flexed but he didn't object—couldn't. I took him deeper and sensation engulfed him. I swirled my tongue over the soft head of his cock and eased my lips up and down his shaft.

Between times, I stroked his balls.

Strange little things mortals are, and the men, so vulnerable, so helpless as the passion takes them. This one was no different.

His hips rocked, his shoulders rose off the bed and his legs stiffened as he neared his climax. He cried out, sweet guttural sounds as the jism rose in his cock and I tasted the sweetness of human life.

I waited to bite until he was lost in the throes of ecstasy. Did he notice? Who can tell with humans? He gasped and called out as his body jerked under my fangs and I milked him of blood and come, drawing on his strength and the abundance of human essence.

When he was spent, I lifted my mouth, wiping it on the sheets before I looked up at him. He was breathing heavily, eyes closed and a smile on his face. He seemed more than content to sleep in my bed, but that I could not permit.

I arose and, donning a satin wrapper, brought him a glass of wine.

"For you," I said, "to restore your strength."

"I have none left," he replied.

Putting my arm behind his shoulders, I eased him to sitting. "Drink deep, *mon brave*," I told him, "the night awaits us both."

He drained the glass and I dressed him, moving fast so he barely noticed what I was doing. No doubt he sensed a breeze or a draft in the room. "Don't you have a home to go to?" I asked, when he was clothed.

"Paris is my home," he replied, "the theaters, the *boites*, the clubs."

Maybe, but he did not inhabit the streets. "I'll walk you back to the club where I found you."

He made some mild protest but since I was tying on my bonnet, he agreed and I walked him back to the smoky club, knowing full well he would not remember the way to my rooms. If indeed he even remembered me. We can take liberties with mortal minds that way.

"What do you do," I asked as we neared a corner near the nightclub, "when you are not downing bottles of wine?"

"I paint Paris, her life and her lovers," he replied.

Another one, but this one had more depth, more passion than most of the would-be artists. A better tailor too. "Farewell, lover of Paris," I told him and disappeared into the arms of the night.

I never saw him again; it does not do to frequent the same mortals, and shortly after I took my little servant with me and left Paris again.

But from time to time over the intervening years, I have thought of that man, his air of despondency, his stunted legs and a most unforgettable cock.

TAKEOUT OR DELIVERY?

Evan Mora

The twenty-first century took some getting used to; it wasn't everyone's cup of tea. Gone were the days of tight-fitting breeches and smart velvet waistcoats, of supple calfskin boots rising nearly to the knee. Gone too were the scores of virginal offerings laced up in colorful dresses that fell demurely to the floor, like the wrappings of so many pretty packages.

James knew that there were those among his kind who lamented the passage of time; who bemoaned the advent of television and rock music, the promiscuity of youth and DNA testing. So much harder these days, they said, to be the romantic vampire of old; no damsels to rescue, no innocents to seduce.

There were others who held fast to a different sort of tradition, refusing to part company with their silk-lined black capes and head-to-toe black vestments. They still favored dramatic pale skin and blood red lips, and reveled in the fear of their victims. But hard times had befallen them too; the shock value of sinister-looking fangs was severely diminished in this era of rampant consumerism, when one need only Google *vampire fangs* to find any one of a hundred purveyors of so-called vampire goods, promising the finest, most realistic custom fangs around.

James felt no sympathy for either of these groups. Adaptability was, of course, key to survival, but more than that, James appreciated the opportunities this new century offered, and had taken to this era like a duck to water.

Two hundred years ago he'd been a strapping young lord of twenty-five, too consumed with getting under the skirts of anything that moved to have given serious attention to career or family, much to his father's dismay. *Handsome as the devil*, women whispered to one another, matrons shaking their heads, young girls giggling behind their hands. But old and young, rich and poor alike, they all welcomed his attentions, whether parting their genteel thighs on beds draped in silks or hoisting their skirts to their waists while braced against scarred tables in the back rooms of taverns.

His appetites did not discriminate; he was as happy with his cock pumping into the mouth of a lusty young scullery maid as he was filling the cunt of a nobleman's lonely wife. Two, three, four times a night his cock could rise, heavy with need and eager for release. He seduced when he needed to, and ravaged the rest with casual disregard.

Thus did Lilith find him—find him and take him for her own. In her he found a hunger that matched his, and the two spent endless nights in a frenzy of coupling, fucking and stroking and licking and sucking their way to release again and again, until Lilith's bed was wet with their mingled sweat and come, and the scent of sex was thick in the air.

One such night, James fell exhausted to the bed, his heart still beating wildly, and Lilith rose from her knees, tongue tracing her swollen lips to capture the last of his seed. She climbed onto the bed, stalking toward him on hands and knees like a hungry she-cat until she straddled his waist, licking the sweat from his skin even as she ground her cunt against his softening cock.

"Lover," she said, her sultry voice more tempting than any siren, "tonight I have need of something more from you."

James chuckled deep in his chest, stroking a hand along the curve of her back till he cupped her bottom possessively.

"In good time woman; give me but a moment to recover," he said.

Lilith purred against his chest, her tongue circling the flat disk of his nipple until it hardened. She nipped the sensitive tissue and James hissed in response, his grip tightening on her ass and his cock stirring beneath her.

"I want you deep inside me, be assured, but that is not the thing of which I speak," she whispered, tongue tracing up the smooth muscle of his chest, teasing the column of his neck.

Teeth replaced tongue, and James moaned at the delicate scrape of her teeth across his heated skin. She teased him to life with the sensuous movements of her body and the erotic workings of her mouth on his throat until he was hot and hard and aching to bury himself in her wet heat again. She lowered herself onto his cock with aching slowness, drawing a moan from his parted lips.

He gripped her hips and thrust upward, trying to penetrate her more deeply and increase their tempo, but she withdrew, holding herself just out of reach, her laughter like the tinkle of bells in his ears. She shook her head, and he understood that the lead this time was hers, and he relaxed as much as he could, waiting to see where she would take them.

Again, she lowered herself onto his cock, taking him in as much as she was able before rising so that only the head of his cock remained inside her. She did this again and again, her hips rising and falling sinuously, her mouth against his neck, teasing him until he couldn't think coherently and his cock throbbed with the need for release. His hands gripped her hips tightly, though he struggled to keep himself still, body trembling with the effort.

Lilith rewarded him by increasing her tempo, her own need rising, fucking him with wanton abandon as their pleasure mounted. James could feel his orgasm building, and the scrape of Lilith's teeth against his neck became more insistent, a pleasurable pain that made him moan. James arched his head back to allow her greater access, and cried out when he felt her teeth penetrate his flesh, his body overwhelmed by the most exquisite pain, orgasm flooding through him with the strength of a tidal wave.

James shuddered in the aftermath of his climax, his limbs leaden, his hands falling away from Lilith's hips to lie uselessly at his side. He thought listlessly that he was cold, and spared a single thought wondering at the cause. At that moment, Lilith rose up above him, his cock still buried in her depths, and she was revealed to him as never before—cheeks flushed, eyes unnaturally bright, elongated canines stained crimson with his blood. Understanding and horror filled James's mind, rising and then fading in a single beat of his sluggish heart. His eyes rolled back in his head and he felt curiously detached from his surroundings.

"Lover," Lilith's voice called him back from the beckoning darkness, "take what I offer, so that you might wake to a night you have never imagined."

James struggled to focus on her face as she pressed something warm to his cold lips. Fluid, rich and hot, filled his mouth and he swallowed without thought, helpless beneath her, bereft of any thought save for Lilith.

Beautiful Lilith.

James awoke with his cock aching and heavy, enveloped by the silken heat of Lilith's mouth. Pleasure thundered through him with an intensity that made all previous experiences fade into nothingness. He felt his canines lengthen and hissed, a feral roar erupting from his chest as his eyes snapped open, revealing the world anew.

For thirty years, he had roamed the world at Lilith's side.

In the beginning, his need for blood had been a clawing, tearing pain that had burned in his veins with each rising, and he had sated that need indiscriminately. He'd lacked grace and finesse, tearing into the throats of his victims with lusty abandon, blood spilling everywhere, moaning with pleasure as hot thick fluid filled his mouth and slid down his throat. Invariably his cock was rock hard, and he'd scarcely have finished feeding before he was opening his breeches and pumping into Lilith's fevered cunt, fucking her with a strength that bordered on violence while she urged him on, licking the blood from his face, whispering in his ear.

In time, she taught him patience; their gifts were many and their prey infinite, and James learned control enough not to kill those from whom he fed, and to remove any memory of himself from their minds.

Lilith also taught him to savor their pleasures.

By day they slept like the dead, wrapped in each other's arms, but by night their lives were filled with wickedness and debauchery. James would seduce a willing bed-partner—perhaps two—holding his bloodlust at bay until they were naked and writhing beneath him with lust. Sometimes Lilith would join him, and the two would feast on an orgy of sex and blood; sometimes she was content to watch, her eyes glittering like twin flames as he buried his cock in eager flesh and sank his teeth deep in their necks.

When the time came for them to part company, Lilith and he did so without sadness. Theirs had been a togetherness born not of love, but of driving hunger, and a thing bound, in time, to fade. James was certain that Lilith was out there even now schooling the raging lusts of a new companion, while he...he was logging on to Lavalife.

James adored the Internet; he thought it a miraculous invention. If one had had the vision (which he did) to have invested in the scores of dot.com companies from their inceptions, one could have made millions upon millions without ever lifting a finger (which he had).

He loved the ridiculous amounts of information that could be had with a simple keystroke. He loved the rampant voyeurism that the Internet allowed—from homemade porn videos to the carefully guarded secrets of the celebrity world. But most of all, James loved the websites that catered to the desires of the lonely and the sexually available, where one could peruse the age, weight, height, hair and eye color and sexual predilections of anyone, anywhere. It was a veritable takeout menu of delights.

In a city like New York, the possibilities were endless. He could select a pretty face, engage in a little witty online flirtation (or sexually explicit conversation, depending on his mood), and his night was set. He'd met women with vampire fetishes who got wet at the sight of his fangs and begged him to bite them as he fucked them; he'd fulfilled secret fantasies of women who wanted violent, anonymous sex in dirty alleyways; he'd been the sensual lover of lonely women who simply craved someone to reach out and hold. And in the end, when he'd sated his cock and drunk his fill of their blood, he carefully erased his presence from their minds, preserving his perfect anonymity.

Logging into his account, James clicked on the site's search engine, scrolling through the list of body attributes and sexual interests he could select. Thinking about Lilith had made him long for something more visceral than a simple seduction. He wanted something hard and intense, bloodletting and slick wetness, a woman trembling with fear and desire and the scent of blood and sex heavy in the air. He selected Domination & Submission, and scrolled through the results.

PrettyKitty...EvilEve...and so on, and so on, and so on. But wait—BlondPrincess... hmm... *Submissive, kinky little blonde. You tell me what to do.* Now that had promise.

James clicked on her profile. Blonde, hazel eyes, five foot five, fit figure. These things mattered little to James, so he skipped to the interesting parts. *Likes: Leather clothing, bondage, being a submissive/slave. What I want in a partner: Aggressiveness, high sex drive, will take control.* Perfect.

James sent a message to BlondePrincess: *You wanna be my slave tonight, little princess?* A minute passed.

Lots of guys talk...can you follow through?

James laughed at her cheek.

I can give you all you can take, and then some, he replied. His cursor blinked as he stared at the screen, awaiting her reply.

I'm hungry tonight. I want you to make me hurt for you—I want it—no—I need it. Anything goes. Can you do that for me?

James smiled viciously. Yes, she'd do nicely.

They spent another twenty minutes messaging back and forth; James said all the things she wanted him to say; he knew this part by heart. All these women really wanted was a basic understanding that he wasn't a hatchet murderer, though they secretly thrilled at the idea that they were doing something a little bit dangerous.

Your place or mine? she wrote. Hmm.... Takeout or delivery?

Mine, he replied. He didn't want the hassle of trying to clean up her apartment afterward, not with what he had in mind. He supplied her with directions and sat back, awaiting her arrival.

The view from James's penthouse loft was the best that money could buy. Though he didn't know what it looked like during the day, James was certain it looked better by night. The entire south wall was floor-to-ceiling glass that framed the Manhattan skyline, shadowy outlines of skyscrapers and a million tiny lights twinkling in the dark. Van Gogh himself couldn't have painted a more beautiful starry night.

James looked out over the city, the room behind him bathed in the muted glow of candlelight. Hunger beat at him, a constant thrum in his veins despite the passage of time. The thought of blood roused a different kind of hunger as well, and his cock stirred with desire. The two had always been inextricably linked for him; his sexual appetites had been what drew Lilith to him, after all.

The buzzer sounded; he didn't bother asking who it was. A few moments passed and then she was there, Amy—the Blonde-Princess, knocking on his door. James opened the door wide, and heard her gasp, though she tried to look casual. He'd answered the door wearing only black leather pants, the chiseled perfection of his smooth chest laid bare for her to see. That was the other thing he liked about this kind of exchange—no need for any preliminaries.

"Amy. Won't you come in?" He gestured to the open space behind him with a broad sweep of his arm.

She stepped over the threshold, and James closed the door quietly behind her. She took a few steps into the room and then stopped, unsure of what to do as James offered no further instruction. Her gaze took in the room and its furnishings before coming to rest on the panoramic views of the glittering city.

"It's beautiful, isn't it?" James's voice was a low purr in her ear. Amy's lips parted with surprise; she hadn't realized he was so close behind her, but she nodded her agreement. James ran sure hands down her arms, over her stomach and under the hem of her shirt, tracing back up over her ribs and cupping her full breasts, massaging her nipples into tight peaks while he ran his tongue experimentally from the hollow beneath her ear to the top of her collarbone.

Amy shuddered and he felt her heart accelerate, scented her arousal mingled with the smallest trace of fear. James's arousal grew in return and he squeezed her breasts more firmly, pinching her nipples between thumb and forefinger and biting down at the juncture of her shoulder and neck, though he was careful not to break the skin. Amy moaned, leaning her head back on his shoulder to allow him greater access. James ground his hips against her ass, the thick length of his arousal straining against its leather confines. Amy's hands caressed his thighs through the soft leather, urging him on, silently communicating her need for more.

James released her breasts and spun her around, his hand knotting painfully in her blonde tresses, holding her still while his mouth slanted across hers, his tongue snaking aggressively into her mouth to slide against her own. He kissed her ruthlessly, bruising her lips under the pressure of his mouth. With his other hand, he unbuttoned the front of her jeans, sliding his palm beneath the waistband of her panties and down, his fingers discovering her wetness and plunging inside. Amy moaned at the dual invasion of mouth and cunt, widening her stance to allow James greater access.

James bit her lower lip and a single bead of blood welled up, quickly captured with a stroke of his tongue. His senses flared, the smell and taste and texture of the sanguine fluid on his tongue an aphrodisiac like no other. He felt his canines lengthen and his cock harden to the point of pain. He released her abruptly and Amy looked down, cheeks flooded with heat, pants undone.

"Do you wish to stay?" He would ask once; no more.

Amy made no answer, but removed her clothing until she was naked in the candlelight. She knelt before him, sitting on her heels with eyes downcast, her hands upturned on her thighs like delicate flowers. In the flickering light, James made out thin, silvery scars that stretched between her shoulder blades and across the tops of her breasts, evidence that Amy was not a stranger to a very different parting of the flesh. He traced the lines on her back gently.

"Stand up," he said.

Amy rose to her feet, but did not look at him. With a fore-finger beneath her chin, James tipped her head up and saw the need and shame in her eyes.

"Do not be ashamed," James said quietly, tracing gentle fingers across the scars on her breasts, "your needs and mine are the same." Amy gasped softly at his meaning.

"Come," he said, taking her hand in his and leading her through his living space until they were but a few feet from the south wall. James had finished his preparations before Amy had arrived, and released a tie that had been nestled unseen among the draperies, allowing a large hook on an industrial chain to be lowered into sight, suspended from the rafters above.

James took a length of black silk from where it had been draped on the arm of his sofa and bound Amy's wrists securely, raising her arms above her head placing the silk bindings on the hook so that the tips of Amy's toes just touched the polished concrete floor. James had prepared a second length of silk as a blindfold, but sensed that it was unnecessary.

James regarded the vision he'd created, drinking in the fragile beauty of the woman stretched and suspended before him, all of New York a glittering backdrop to the canvas he was painting. Amy moaned softly, eyes closed as her body adjusted to its minor discomforts. In the glow of the candlelight, Amy's skin took on a beautiful golden hue, her stomach taut, breasts thrust forward, muscles in her calves and thighs straining as she struggled to stay on tiptoes.

James stroked her body with sure hands, testing the weight of her breasts in his palms, teasing her nipples into hard peaks once more before moving lower, kneading the supple flesh of her ass, reaching between her thighs to stroke her pussy, urging her legs further apart. He dipped his fingers into her heat, coating them with her fluids and drawing them forward so that he bathed her clit with her wetness, alternately stroking and pinching her most sensitive flesh until she was whimpering with arousal, trying to grind herself onto the hand that was the source of both her pleasure and pain.

James continued to torment her body, but added his mouth, suckling her breasts, biting her nipples until she moaned with supplication, then bathing the tiny hurts with his tongue. He did this again and again, each time increasing the pressure of his mouth, his own arousal raging, until it was all he could do not to tear into the tender flesh and spill her blood right then. He stepped away from her, and Amy cried out in earnest, body writhing with need.

"Look at me," James commanded, and she did, focusing on him and stilling her body.

"See me for what I am," he said, and Amy took in his unnaturally bright eyes, which seemed almost to glow in the dimly lit room. His lips were parted slightly, and his canines were clearly visible, sharp and deadly.

James circled her slowly, passing in and out of her vision, stalking her like a predator. The scent of her fear rose, mingling with her arousal, but despite this she said nothing. James stopped in front of her, his eyes searching hers and finding only need— need for sex…and blood. James felt a kinship with her he'd not felt in too many cold, hungry decades.

He moved quickly—too quickly for her to register or flinch— his fingers curved like talons as they slashed across her chest. Amy's head arched back, thrusting her torso into the pain with a sharp cry. Four thin lines appeared above her left breast, blood welling quickly and spilling down over her breast and belly.

James slashed again, and a matching set of lines appeared above her right breast, bright crimson against the cream of her skin. Amy's wail was low and sustained, her release a tangible force moving through her body as her blood flowed, tears seeping from beneath thick lashes, intense shudders wracking her body.

James traced reverent fingers through her blood, breathed in its rich, coppery scent and lapped it from her skin. He removed his pants with quick efficiency, the urgency of his desire unable to wait any longer. He positioned himself between her thighs and lifted her onto his cock, sliding into her easily, her cunt slick with the evidence of her pleasure.

He thrust into her hungrily, taking her mouth at the same time, blood and sweat pooling between their bodies, their lips and tongues entwined. He broke the kiss, dipping his head to bathe the shallow cuts with his tongue, moaning at the heady taste of her in his mouth.

"James…" she whispered, drawing his attention back to her, capturing his eyes and arching her head back in invitation, the smooth expanse of her throat laid bare to his hunger.

James didn't hesitate, sinking his teeth deep in her tender flesh, the explosion of blood in his mouth like touching a live wire. Amy's hoarse cry of release barely registered, her body rocking with the force of the orgasm tearing through her, cunt spasming around his cock as his hips pistoned into her, his own climax leaving him spent and trembling in its wake.

James gently lifted Amy, releasing her arms and cradling her weak and sleepy frame against his chest. He carried her to his bathroom, sitting on the edge of the tub with her in his lap while he ran a warm bath, massaging her arms to get the blood circulating in those tissues again. Amy murmured sleepily when he lowered her into the water, but she continued to drift somewhere between sleep and wakefulness, her eyes never opening as James bathed the blood from her skin and tended to her wounds.

When he was satisfied that the bleeding had stopped he toweled her off, carefully dressing her, then himself, before guiding her to his car, politely asking her address and driving her home, depositing her in her bed before letting himself out.

She'd wake in the morning with cloudy memories of the night before, bearing very visible reminders of the night's activities, though she'd be embarrassed that she could remember neither the face nor the name of her mystery lover, or the exact manner in which the marks had been obtained.

James drove into the night with a smile on his face—she was definitely going on his Hotlist.

DEVOURING HEART

Andrea Dale

The music throbbed, a heavy beat that spoke of dark things. Dark things that, like the music, got under your breastbone and lodged there, pressing rhythmically against your heart. Most of the lights in the club were red, making everyone look as though he or she had been doused with fresh blood.

It was like being inside a pulsating heart. I moved through it, aorta and ventricle and life-affirming beats, looking for Sorcha.

Sorcha first walked into the club two years ago. I remember the night, of course. Everyone turned to stare, because she was gorgeous, with straight, blue-streaked black hair down to her ass. Said ass was delectable, covered in a leather miniskirt over ripped fishnets. She wore a white baby-doll top that depicted a mouth biting into a broken heart. The shirt was skintight and a size too small, revealing a slice of pouty tummy and outlining a pair of pierced nipples.

I wanted nothing more than to rub my own breasts against those cold rings, to wrap my hands around her tight ass and grind my crotch against hers until we were both screaming incoherently.

But first, I wanted to ask her to dance.

I didn't believe in love at first sight. I'm still not sure I do, not even now. It took me a couple of months to fall in love with her, or so I tell myself. That first night, however, when she walked in, and everybody stared, and everybody wanted her...it didn't matter.

She walked straight up to me.

Dancing was just exquisite, excruciating foreplay for us. Two or three songs later, her pierced tongue was licking my earlobe in time to the driving beat of the music, making me imagine what that would feel like against my clit, which pulsed in the same rhythm. Her hands proved to me that my belly ring made that area a huge erogenous zone for me.

I soared and swam in a sea of scarlet desire.

I took her home that night, and fulfilled those fantasies I was having and then some. Playing with her nipple piercings was enough to make her come, and we discovered her hands were small enough to fit inside of me. When she uncurled her fist in my slippery cunt, my vision bloomed roses, red and black.

I'd had my share of one-night stands, and I told myself I didn't expect her to be much more than that. I'd be happy if she stuck around, but I didn't dare hope for it. At the end of the night, she told me she loved me. When I asked her how that was possible, she said, "I didn't know I was looking for anyone, but when I walked in and I saw you, I just *knew*."

Two years later, it was my turn to walk in looking for her. Because five days ago, she'd disappeared.

I didn't see her anywhere, but it was hard to see through the crush of dancing bodies. I mounted the industrial metal steps up to the bar, where I'd have a better view.

Ambrose, looking dashing as usual in a tuxedo top made out of strips of black and white leather with a bow tie of spikes, handed me a double shot of vodka before I asked. I drank it in one gulp, without a shudder. I couldn't taste anything these days.

"I'm sorry, Case, but you missed her," he said. "She left maybe half an hour ago."

I nodded my thanks to him, paid double what I owed, and left. Outside, I threw the shot glass against the wall, but the sound of shattering glass didn't help. Then I went to Sorcha's house.

She hadn't bothered to lock the front door, not that I couldn't have picked the lock if necessary. I'd done it before, these past five days, to find the place empty. I'd even waited inside all one night, creeping out just before dawn.

If my actions screamed "Stalker!" or "Crazed ex-lover!" I didn't fucking care, okay? Maybe even crazy stalkers think they have their reasons, think it's all for the best.

They were in the bedroom, and from the moans of ecstasy, I assumed they were having sex. No reason not to, I supposed. I flipped on the light—Sorcha favored blue bulbs, and it was like peering through a bottle of curaçao, or swimming in a Caribbean sea (not that I'd ever see that). Sorcha was wearing the sapphire satin corset I'd bought her. My gut wrenched, aching more than I expected it to.

Her partner's head shot up, but Sorcha was slower to move, languidly disengaging her teeth from the other woman's wrist.

"Case," she said. She sounded drunk. That's the sensation vampires feel when they're feeding. I'd guessed what had happened to her when she disappeared, and Ambrose had confirmed my suspicions three days ago. If you hang out long enough at the club, you'll get approached with an offer. Not everybody takes it, and I was surprised—stunned—that Sorcha had.

I grabbed the other woman—whose mouth was blood-wet, so I knew she'd already fed—and threw her at the bedroom door. The jamb splintered when she slammed against it.

"Get the fuck out," I snarled. She pulled herself upright and snarled incoherently back, but she left. I heard the front door bang shut.

"Case," Sorcha said again.

"Sorcha, you idiot," I said, kneeling on the bed next to her. "Why didn't you tell me?"

"I was afraid, Case," she said, and I heard the desperation in her voice. "I didn't want—I don't want—"

"Never mind," I said, still with a snarl in my voice. "Just shut up and fuck me."

Our coupling was as violent and incredible as our first. I yanked her sweet breasts out from the corset before she knew what hit her, and I straddled her thigh and used the nipple rings like reins. I rode her, but in truth I wasn't after my own gratification—not yet, at least.

Did I want to punish her for running away from me? Maybe, a little. Punishment for Sorcha was pleasure, so it wasn't as if I was teaching her a lesson.

I couldn't deny her. My knee wedged between her legs but it almost wasn't needed, because she could come just from the way I twisted and tugged the piercings. Her nipples flushed near-purple, and she bucked beneath me, writhing in pain that transmuted into pleasure and back again.

"It's okay," I whispered, my lips pressed against the pulse in her neck.

After that first round of orgasms she had recovered from the feeding and was stronger, so I let her take control. ("It's okay," she'd whispered back, and I'd believed her.) She buckled leather cuffs—blue, like her corset—around my wrists. The cheap gold spray paint had worn away from the wooden headboard where the cuffs had been chained time and time again.

She strapped on our favorite black dildo and thrust it toward my mouth—black dildo, blue satin, blurring into a bruise as I sucked. She knew what I wanted, what I would have begged for if she hadn't been gagging me with the silicone cock, and that was to have it inside me, to have her leaning over me, sweaty and flushed, while she plunged it into me.

But even when she did, she teased and toyed—and restrained, I could do nothing but force my hips harder toward hers, struggling for satisfaction. It wasn't our usual game, but I was so happy to have found her again that even the frustration was mixed with a contradictory sense of relief.

Still, when she pulled the dildo out of me, I swore at her, nasty terms of endearment. She smiled, just a little, as she promised me what I'd been begging for.

She slid a smaller vibrating cock into my ass and slid her face down my body, I assumed to lick my aching clit. Instead she tongued my belly piercing, and I arched my back as best I could, and that's when she pressed another vibrator to my clit. Then all I knew was that I shattered and screamed and ultimately came very, very close to passing out. When I thought I couldn't bear to come anymore, I begged her to stop, insisting I would die even though we both knew that couldn't happen.

She undid one of the cuffs so I could tuck an arm around her before she fell asleep on my chest. Exhausted, sated, finally back in her arms, I followed her into oblivion.

Which showed just how irrationally desperate I was for a happy ending. As always, I should have known better.

I woke to the sandpaper rasp of teeth scraping my neck. I sighed my contentment; so this was what she wanted, after all.

But she'd barely broken the skin before she pulled away, sobbing.

"Sorcha?" I reached out my free hand.

"I'm sorry, Case, but I can't do it. I can't bring you down into this. I know it sounds like the perfect life: never aging, never dying, feasting in the dark." She gave a bark of humorless laughter. "The perfect goth fantasy. But it's not. The killing makes me sick. The drinking is…abhorrent to me. It's disgusting. I can't make you do that, too. I love you, and I want you with me always, but I can't let you suffer with me."

She ran out of the bedroom. A moment later, I saw the bright crack of light between the heavy curtains, and realized it was full morning.

"Sorcha, no!"

I wrenched at the cuff, now a prison, until I heard the headboard crack and splinter. I was halfway down the stairs when Sorcha opened the door. I screamed her name again, and she turned.

"I love you," she said, and stepped backward into the sunlight and died.

I spent the rest of the day in her house, trapped. I lost count of how many times I walked up to that open door and stood there, looking out.

I'd known what had happened to her in those five missing days, and I'd allowed the same thing to happen to me, so we could be together always.

She never gave me the chance to tell her.

But I couldn't bring myself to step outside. Sorcha, in the end, was far braver than I could ever be.

WICKED KISSES

Michelle Belanger

The vampire circled her, its azure eyes glittering in the lamp-
light. It was tall and sleek, with the shapely form of a
woman—although she had been told that the vampires didn't
recognize gender. It was just a cunning camouflage to make their
species blend better with its prey. This didn't stop Alita from
finding the woman desperately attractive, but apparently this
was a part of their camouflage as well. All vampires were sexy,
even though sex was not what they sought from mortals. For
vampires, it was all about blood, and everyone had that.

Still, all of the books she had read suggested that vampires
had a fondness for pretty things. She had taken special measures
to make herself as pretty as possible. With her long, shapely legs
and her warm, almond-colored skin, Alita knew she was attractive. Nevertheless, she had primped and preened the whole day,
preparing for this momentous occasion. She wore a long flowing
gown of lustrous green silk. She had selected the fabric specifi-
cally to match her eyes. The skirt was slit up both legs, allowing

easy access to the tender flesh of her inner thighs. She had left off any necklaces or bracelets, wanting to keep the preferred targets of wrist and neck bare. She would have swept back her long fall of straight black hair as well, but vanity prevented her. She loved the way her hair flowed like an ebony river down her back—loved it too much to pin up even for the convenience of a vampire lover.

The female vampire (it seemed too impersonal to refer to her as "it," gender or no gender) continued to prowl carefully around her with feline grace. Alita knew that there was a ritual to be observed. Approach the temple. Ring the bell. Stand in the darkened antechamber, then wait. When she had first arrived, not even the butter lamps had been lit. And then it seemed as if they lit themselves. Shortly thereafter, this desperately beautiful woman appeared, but she did not immediately approach. Instead, she behaved like she was stalking Alita, feeling her out. Perhaps she was testing the girl's nerves. But Alita had waited too long for this. There was no chance that she was going to get intimidated and run away. She squeezed the little token in her palm, drawing strength from its sleek, red-lacquered shape. This was her ticket and her talisman, the auspicious lot that would declare to all that she had earned her place.

The vampire's lips were full and pouting from the pressure of her distended fangs. A moment later, she smiled, and Alita stared at the wickedly sharp canines. They were long and thin like a snake's. She had expected fangs that looked more like those of a cat, or perhaps a wolf. But these looked needle sharp, the better for piercing tender skin. The mere thought sent shivers of anticipation cascading down the backs of Alita's legs.

After the vampire had made its seventh pass, Alita knew that it was time. She had been given seven chances to change her mind and flee. Seven, and she had stood her ground. Now it was her turn to take part in this ancient play. She held out the lot in her upturned palm, making certain that the vampire could see.

"I won," she said, more breathily than she had intended. "The lot fell to me."

The vampire's jewel-like eyes flicked from the chip to her face and then back again. Spring-taut muscles relaxed and she bowed her head to Alita.

"You are the Scarlet One," the being declared. "You have earned the right to come in from the outside and enter the sacred chambers of our temple."

Alita loosed a breath she had not realized she had been holding. The vampire cocked her head. "You are certain you come willingly?"

Alita felt herself trembling all over, but it was not from fear. She knew what was coming, and her body yearned for it in ways that made her feel like she was melting from the inside out. She couldn't tell the vampire this; it was not a part of the protocol. So she tried to master her hunger and meet the predator's sapphire gaze calmly and evenly.

"I come willingly," Alita declared.

The vampire bowed its head again, then smiled. Faster than Alita could react, the creature stepped behind her, nuzzling its face into her thick black hair. Alita could feel the vampire's breath on her throat, and she bit down on her lip, desperate for what would come next. The vampire's lips lightly grazed the skin over her jugular, and Alita felt the pulse throb in response. She stifled a little cry, trying to swallow it deep in her throat, but could not stop herself from trembling.

She did not even realize that she had been leaning into the vampire's embrace until the being stepped away as swiftly as it had stepped behind her. Still leaning, Alita almost lost her footing and fell. She blushed furiously with embarrassment, hanging her head so that her dark hair would swing forward and veil her reddened cheeks.

Standing before her again, the vampire held out one hand. The nails on its fingers were sharp and curved, yet flawlessly manicured. "Come with me to the chamber."

Alita reached out and let the vampire close chilly fingers around her wrist. The grip was firm but gentle, and it thrilled the girl to know that the creature could have crushed the bones of her wrist to powder on a whim. Instead, the predator led her into the shadows that engulfed most of the antechamber. Alita was dimly aware of other humanlike forms shifting in the dark. She had neither heard them nor felt their eyes upon her during her previous exchange, and yet they must have been there the entire time, quietly observing.

She was led deeper into the temple, down shadowed halls, with only the grip of cool fingers on her wrist as a guide. Alita tried not to stumble, trusting herself completely to the predators who undoubtedly trailed silently behind her in the darkness.

Finally, she was led to a room with a huge canopy bed draped in silks of scarlet. Like the other room, it was bigger than the pool of candlelight that illuminated it. Alita knew that here, too, silent predators waited in the shadows. She didn't fixate on their mute and hidden presences. Instead, awestruck, she let her eyes glide along the gorgeous bed with its heavy, bronze frame. This was the bed of the Scarlet Ones, and, in another day and age, it was also an altar of sacrifice. Had the lot fallen to her a thousand years before, she would never have lived to see another sunrise. But the vampires had grown crafty through the years. They learned the wisdom of keeping their willing prey alive, and thus the lottery had changed. It was no longer mandatory. Instead, it had become a coveted privilege. Only the best and most beautiful youths and maidens could apply for a chance to be selected, and even then, they were limited to applying but once a year. Stories were told throughout the land of the decadence and sensuality of the vampires' temple. The Scarlet Ones were beloved providers, kept as companions and pets, wanting for nothing.

Alita had dreamed her whole life of the sensual luxury of this temple. For this moment, she had made herself beautiful, cultivating an exoticism that she was certain would catch the eye of even the most inhuman of the vampires.

She gazed with expectant longing at the creature who had escorted her through the twisting halls that no humans from the outside world would ever see—no human who was not a Scarlet One, as she was now. The being, more beautiful than a demigod, released Alita's wrist and gestured to the legendary bed.

"Lie back and be comfortable," the vampire said.

Alita obeyed immediately, reverently approaching the bed and positioning herself in the very middle of it. The mattress was deep and soft, and the entire surface was covered with little beaded pillows. The jade silk of her dress shimmered pleasingly against the scarlet silk of the sheets, and Alita tossed her head back, splaying her onyx tresses across the pillows. As she situated herself upon the bed, her vampire escort disappeared soundlessly into the darkness. Alita had the illusion of being in the chamber alone, at least for a few minutes.

Then, with stealthy movements, but still making more sound than their inhuman guardians, a pair of mortal attendants emerged from the shadows on one side of the room. Their exceptional beauty as well as their scarlet robes declared them past winners of the same coveted privilege that Alita herself now claimed.

One of the servants was male and one was female. Neither looked much older than Alita herself. They each had long, flowing hair and dusky skin and they looked similar enough that they could have passed for brother and sister. They wore no jewelry or other adornments, save for their flowing silk robes.

They bore a tray between them, laden with sponges, scented oil, a ewer and a matching silver bowl. Moving as one, they set the tray down near where Alita lay, and silently they set to work sponging her flesh with the cool, scented water. They gestured for her to remove her dress, a development she had not expected. She hadn't worn anything underneath, hoping there were some exceptions to the rumors that vampires never engaged in conventional sex with humans. The attendants lifted her dress off, secreting it away in a compartment under the bed. Then, from the same compartment, they produced a pair of razors. Beckoning for Alita to lie back and relax, they snicked away all the hair that blossomed between her thighs with sure, swift movements. Although the two were passionless and efficient in their work, Alita found the process impossibly erotic. As one held the delicate folds of her inner flesh apart so the other could drag a razor across every surface, her arousal mounted until she could no longer bear it. She arched back against the pillows, loosing a shuddering sigh as her pleasure peaked and then achieved a gentle, rolling release. She came two more times before they were finished, but if they noticed or even cared, they gave no sign.

Focused on the task at hand, they sponged her and shaved her, and then they poured shimmering oil into their strong, deft hands. Working in unison, they rubbed the scented oil over her lithe, young body until her skin had a luster that reflected the glow of the candle flames. Wiping the oil from their hands, the silent pair arranged her on the pillows, fanning her hair out artfully so it splayed around her head like a crown.

After arranging her glowing, naked form on the scarlet sheets of the bed, the pair gathered up their tools and withdrew. The room was silent for a time, and just as Alita was growing restless, someone nearby lit incense. It drifted in lazy whorls, immersing the whole room in a languorous haze. The aromatic incense was spicy and sweet by turns, with notes of amber, clove, and vanilla. There must have been something more potent in the incense as well, because soon Alita felt herself drifting on a luscious cloud of scent and sensation. Dreamily, she ran her fingers up and down the supple folds of the silk sheets, awash in sensuality. Her pulse throbbed in her freshly shaved labia, and her nipples speared the air.

In the depths of the temple, someone began tolling a bell. It was deep-throated and sonorous, and its slow, steady rhythm evoked answering vibrations from places deep within Alita's already throbbing flesh. She rubbed and chafed her thighs together, not daring to touch herself for fear of offending the vampires she knew were lurking in the nearby shadows. They would touch her, soon enough.

She hardly noticed them when they came, so completely was she set adrift by the sensual feast of incense, silk, and her own flesh. But then their hands were upon her, their chilly fingers tracing patterns upon her warm and scented flesh. The cold was not displeasing to Alita. It was just another sensation in a sea of carnal input. As they ran cold fingertips and sharp claws along Alita's arms and breasts and thighs, little frissons of pleasure shuddered through her, carrying her even farther out to sea.

Their mouths were hot when they tasted her, as hot as their fingertips were cold. The mix of sensations alone almost sent her, but the real climax came when they finally bit deep into her skin. Sharp and sweet they were, those wicked little kisses all over her flesh. She half imagined that they were injecting her with some heady narcotic, the pleasure was so immediate and so intense. But they weren't putting things into her, they were taking things out—sweet scarlet ribbons of life-giving blood. She felt her insides turning to molten gold as the vampires lapped and sucked at her flesh. The wet, hot stream of glowing pleasure trickled down her body to coalesce in the throbbing pulse between her thighs.

All too soon it was over. With final, gentle kisses at each of her wounds, the vampires licked away the last scarlet droplets and then withdrew. Alita felt so light, so completely free, that she simply lay and basked in the sensation. The brother and sister–like attendants returned with fresh sponges and water. They washed her again as she lay there, still half drifting on that sea of immortal passion. They had a tin of something pungent, and this they applied to each of her wounds. It had a sharp yet pleasant scent, and it left her skin warm and tingling wherever they dabbed it. She was hardly surprised when she felt their hands rubbing the same unguent into her newly shaved labia. She thought she was spent after the vampires' attentions, but this roused whole new tides of sensation in her belly and her sex.

She gasped a little when the male of the pair entered her, and then she surprised herself by finding the strength to wrap her legs around his hips and drive him even deeper. She threw her head back into the pillows, nearly screaming with the need to be filled deeply, completely, and immediately. The sister of the pair took full advantage of her open mouth, bending down and snaking her tongue along the inside of Alita's teeth. Alita answered her kiss eagerly, tasting echoes of the pungent salve in the other woman's mouth. There was a faint hint of brine on her breath as well, and Alita wondered whether she had felt only their hands on her delicate nether flesh. And then it didn't matter anymore, because she was coming. The dam burst within her and she was drowned in a shattering wave of orgasms.

The three of them lay tangled together on the scarlet sheets. Kissed and petted and caressed and filled, Alita was lulled to sleep, to dream of sharp, wicked kisses.

FOURTH WORLD

Lisabet Sarai

arry! This is bloody brilliant! Not at all what I had imagined."

I'm gratified by my friend's appreciation, though I expected it. We're sitting at the glass and stainless steel bar at Scirroco, a swank eatery atop one of Bangkok's tallest skyscrapers. The city sprawls fifty stories below us, a jewel-sprinkled tapestry split by the winding black ribbon of the Chao Phaya. Bright sparks flit along that blackness like fireflies, party boats heading up the river, barges drifting down.

A trio plays muted jazz in the corner. Waiters in immaculate white glide among the diners, delivering dishes too artfully presented to consume. I sip my twenty-dollar glass of merlot, which is almost worth the price. Life is good.

"There's more to Bangkok than temples and bar girls, mate. But we can spend tomorrow night in Patpong, if you'd like."

"I want to see it all. Experience everything Thailand has to offer. The highs and the lows. Though I have to say I didn't expect—this—from a third world country."

"Not exactly third world. An Aussie friend of mine says that Thailand is 'fourth world'—a world where laws and logic are indefinitely suspended. Where anything can happen, and usually does. It's a surprising place. Even after three years, I'm still surprised sometimes."

I know what Jeremy was expecting: cheap beer, glaring neon, rock and roll; dusky, scantily clad women greeting him in sing-song English—nothing like the elegant beauty at the other end of the bar, who's eyeing us with undisguised interest.

She has the oval face and almond eyes of a Thai, but her complexion is pale as milk. Jet black hair cascades down her bare back to her waist. Gold encircles her throat and sparkles in her earlobes. Her scarlet dress is a shocking contrast to her white shoulders. The V-shaped neckline offers a glimpse of shadowy cleavage. The silk drapes and reveals her curves, alluring without being too obvious. My cock stirs, sensing possibilities.

Her eyes meet mine. She understands. She slips off her perch and approaches us, wineglass clasped between her finger and thumb. "Good evening, gentlemen," she murmurs. She has only the slightest accent. "May I buy you another round?" With impossible grace, she settles onto the tall stool on the other side of Jeremy and crosses her perfect legs. The gold straps of her high-heeled sandals cradle her slender instep. Her toenails exactly match her dress.

"You're the lady. We should be treating you," I manage to stammer.

"Don't you believe in equal rights for women?" Her laugh is low and musical. She waves a finger at the bartender, and two goblets appear, brimming with ruby liquid. "In any case, you are visitors, aren't you? I want to welcome you to Bangkok."

"Jeremy's visiting me from London, but I live here. For more than three years."

"Really? I've never seen you at Scirroco before." Her eyes are literally black, gleaming in the tastefully dim light. I feel transparent. I know she can see my desire.

"I can't afford to come here all that often. But tonight we're celebrating."

"Aha." She sips her wine. A drop glistens on her scarlet-painted lips. Her tongue flicks out to whisk it away. No one speaks. My cock swells, pulsing inside my briefs. Could she be a working girl? It seems unlikely, given her clothes, her jewelry and her English. Her class. But in Bangkok, anything's possible.

"Your English is amazingly good." I have to say something. Her stare is destroying me. Meanwhile Jeremy is completely tongue-tied.

"My boyfriend from England taught me."

"You have a boyfriend?" What's her game? I realize that I've been leaning toward her. I sit up straight.

"He died already."

"Oh—I'm so sorry." Jeremy finally speaks up. He looks genuinely concerned. He believes her. I want to kick him, but that would be too obvious.

"Never mind." She places her hand on top of Jeremy's. Jeremy is fair, but his skin looks bronzed in comparison to hers. "It was a long time ago. So—Jeremy? What do you think of Thailand so far?"

"I just got here. Around six a.m. this morning. I'm still pretty groggy."

"I can show you things that you'll never read about in your guidebook." She's trailing her flame-tipped fingers up and down Jeremy's bare arm. She licks her lips again. Jeremy can't look away from her. "Would you like to come back to my place?"

"Now?" I interject. I don't want Jeremy getting into trouble. I want her, but I don't trust her.

"Why not? It's a bit noisy in here for a conversation, don't you think?"

I swallow my snort of laughter, knowing that it would be rude. With its background jazz and the hushed murmur of conversations, this may be the only place in the city that's not overly loud.

"We don't want to impose..." I begin.

"Please." She turns those bottomless eyes from my friend to me. My resistance melts as my cock freezes solid. "I insist. I have a very nice bottle of Côtes du Rhone in my cellar that I think you'd both enjoy. I've been saving it for a special occasion."

Her cellar? I don't know what to think. Meanwhile, she assumes that the discussion is over. She lays her Amex Platinum card on the bar. "I'm Mai, by the way."

"Like silk?"

"Oh, do you speak Thai—?"

"Harry. Only a bit. Everyone uses English at the bank where I work. But I know a few words."

"Never mind. I can understand you perfectly." She signs the chit with a flourish. Sliding off the stool, she takes my left arm and Jeremy's right. "Come with me, Jeremy and Harry."

She keeps her body pressed against ours in the lift. To my surprise she hits the button for the car park. I'd assumed that we would take a cab. The trip down takes forever. I find it difficult to breath. Surreptitiously, I check the mirror. Is my boner visible?

Her eyes meet mine in the glass. Her full lips curl into a knowing smile. There's something odd about her reflection. It wavers, flickering in and out of focus. I shake my head and the effect disappears. I must be more drunk than I thought.

As we exit from the lift lobby, still arm in arm in arm, a monstrous black Mercedes glides up to the curb. The door swings open. "Get in, please," she purrs. I slide across the tooled leather, impressed despite myself. Mai, in the middle, cuddles up to me. She pulls Jeremy closer. The automobile floats up the helical ramp and out of the garage, nearly silent. There's a tinted glass barrier. I can't see the driver. Mai flicks her tongue over my earlobe, sending a bolt of lightning to my groin, then makes a wet trail down the side of my neck.

I smell her perfume, jasmine edged with something sharper, less sweet. My heart slams against my ribs. "Who are you?" She must be someone's daughter or wife, a general or a politician. Or maybe the latest pop sensation, though her classic style argues that she's older than her body would suggest.

"I'm nobody. Just a woman looking for a good time. *Sanuk sabai*. You understand?"

"Yes, but…"

"Hush, Harry. You talk too much. You should be more like your friend. A man of action."

I turn to see Jeremy's hand wandering up her silk-clad thigh. I'm surprised by his daring. Back at school he was always the shy one in our crowd. I was the one who took the initiative.

His eyes are closed, his lips parted. His trousers rise up from his groin in an imposing peak. Mai cups his bulk and squeezes. Jeremy groans. His hand slips under her skirt.

Jealousy sizzles through me. A red mist clouds my vision. "Never mind," says Mai, her hand on my thigh, her lips fastening on mine.

Her kiss claims me. I try to take control, to thrust my tongue between her ripe lips, but she playfully forces me back, then plunders my mouth with her own. She tastes sweet but strange, the fruity remnants of her wine not quite hiding a metallic element. My cock surges, painful and eager, trapped in my tight briefs.

Blinded by the fall of her hair around my face, I grope for her breast. Her flesh is firm and elastic under my fingers. Her nipple juts through the flimsy barrier of her dress. I circle it with my thumb and she moans into my mouth. I pinch the delightful nub and she bites my lip, hard enough to draw blood. I want to protest, to push her away, but she's far stronger than I expect. Her kiss becomes more heated, more desperate. My pierced lip throbs. Something's not right, I think, but then her hand settles on my cock and all thought vanishes.

Her fingers skitter across the distorted fabric of my trousers, testing my hardness. She settles her palm over my swollen bulk, squeezing in time with her sucking kisses. I feel the tightening heaviness that tells me I'm going to come. I take a deep breath, trying to gain some control. Her scent floods my nostrils. The need for release overwhelms me. The first spurt of come pulses halfway up my shaft, but then she removes her hand. The urge subsides, becomes just bearable. Her lips graze my earlobe. "Not yet, darling. Save that for me."

Mai sits back, her hand still resting on my thigh. I see that Jeremy's fly is down, his cock poking out. She trails her fingertips across the ruddy bulb. He shudders with obvious desire. "Put that away for now, Jeremy. We've arrived."

My friend blushes as he struggles to stuff his rigid dick back into his pants. I peer through the smoky-colored window and recognize the profile of her exclusive condo building from the newspaper ads. In this building, the price per square meter is four times my monthly salary.

I feel woozy and disoriented, as if I were the one who had just gotten off the fifteen-hour flight. In the lift, Mai descends on poor Jeremy, swallowing him in one of her all-consuming kisses.

She grinds her pelvis against his, hooks one leg around his body
to pull him closer.

Her skirt hikes up to display an endless expanse of snowy
nakedness. Jeremy's hand grips that luscious flesh. I can see the
indentations of his fingernails. They rock together, dry humping,
while I watch helplessly.

My cock strains in my pants, demanding release. I can't
remember ever having wanted someone so much. I want to grab
her, to pull her off my friend and force her back against the
paneled wall. I need to crumple that scarlet silk around her waist
and bury my aching cock in the tight, hot cunt I know I'll find
underneath. I have to have her. If I have to wait any longer, I'll
explode.

Yet I don't move. I can't. I watch the ballet of their entwined
bodies, trapped in some weird lethargy, my lust seething but my
muscles so relaxed I must lean against the wall to support myself.
The lift shoots toward the summit, smooth and silent. I wouldn't
even know that we were moving if not for the progress of the
LED numerals toward the *P* she pressed when we entered.

The lift door slides open. Mai and Jeremy untangle themselves. Mai laughs a little when she sees my obvious distress.
"Don't worry, darling. You'll get your turn."

She takes my arm and helps me out of the lift. Energy flows
back into my limbs, but my mind stays fuzzy. And my cock stays
painfully hard.

Her penthouse is incredible: teak floors and rosewood furniture, jade dragons and golden Buddhas. Mai kicks off her heels
at the door and pads barefoot across the parquet to open the
raw silk drapes. A wall of glass reveals the glittering towers of
the new Bangkok. The skytrain winds round a corner, many
stories below. Off in the distance sparkles the graceful catenary
of the Rama IX bridge.

"Who are you?" I whisper again. None of this seems real. Jeremy stares out into the night, transfixed by the view.

"Just Mai," she says with a smile that breaks my heart. "Nobody." She slips the straps of her dress from her shoulders. It settles into a blood-colored pool at her feet. Naked now, she flips the dress into a corner. "For tonight, your lover. And you will be my lovers."

She holds out her arms to us, to both of us. We scramble madly, tearing off our clothing, unbearably eager to possess that succulent white flesh. She laughs at our awkwardness, but her voice is kind as she welcomes us into her arms.

"I do love handsome boys like the two of you. I've always preferred fair young men—like you, Jeremy." She bends to take one of his nipples in her mouth. He gasps. "You blush so easily. Your blood is so close to the surface." She pinches the nipple with her crimson nails, breaking the skin. A ruby droplet appears on Jeremy's chest. Mai's tongue flicks out to gather it into her mouth.

A shiver runs down my spine. The gesture is unbearably erotic.

"But dark, virile hunks like you are attractive, too." Her fingernails graze my cock lightly, then dig deeper. The pain is minor compared to the flash of pleasure that sears me. She feels the surge as I harden further. "You like a little pain, Harry? Are you kinky, then?"

She leads us both off in the direction of the bedroom. "I have just the thing for you."

"No, not really, I don't think..." At the back of my fuzzy brain, there's a flicker of alarm, but lust drowns it out. It seems that I couldn't resist her even if I wanted to. I'm limp as pudding—except for my cock.

She pushes us both down on the king-sized bed. The silk

sheets feel amazing against my bare butt. She climbs onto the bed, between our prone bodies. I can smell her musk, faint behind the bitter tang of her perfume.

She leans over to fasten her hot mouth on mine. Her tongue squirms against my palate. Her teeth rake my lips. Her breasts swing against my chest, tempting and ripe. I reach up to fondle the firm, resilient globes. She hums in approval.

"Hands above your head, Harry," she directs, breaking the kiss. I'm in some kind of swoon. I obey without thinking. She clasps my wrists in the restraints attached to the headboard. They're lined with padded satin, comfortable, arousing. In Mai's presence, everything is arousing.

She licks her way down my chest, swirling her agile tongue around my rampant penis. It jumps at her touch. I arch, trying to work the tip between her lips, but she pulls back.

"Just a moment, now. I've got to make Jeremy comfortable."

My friend moans when she kisses him. He sighs when she binds him. Another drop of blood has seeped from the tiny wound in his nipple. She laps it up eagerly on her way down to tease his cock.

Mai sits back on her heels. She grips our cocks roughly, making us squirm. "Lovely," she purrs. "Two gorgeous young studs at my command. Who wants to go first?"

Me! Take me! I want to cry, but something holds me back.

"Jeremy's the one on holiday. I think I'll take him first. Are you ready?"

He nods. Speech has deserted him as well. Mai straddles him and lowers her body, painting his knob with her pussy juice. Jeremy moans and jerks his hips upward. The diabolical beauty pulls away before he can enter her. "Now darling, I'm the one in charge. You just relax and have a good time."

Jeremy sinks back onto the bed. Mai repositions her cunt and lowers herself onto his cock, swallowing his length inch by inch.

"Ah..." He looks as though he's going to explode any instant. I'm holding on to control by a hair myself, just watching her play with him. She tenses, obviously contracting her inner muscles. He moans again, louder than before.

Mai lays a finger on his lips. "Don't come yet, little boy. I want you to last a long, long time." Her finger meanders down over his chin, tracing the line of his throat, down between his erect nipples. As it travels, she increases the pressure. I can see the indentation of her sharp fingernail. By the time she reaches his solar plexus, a red trail follows the finger's progress. Very slowly, she slices through the skin of his belly, centimeter by centimeter, watching his face. He seems to be in ecstasy.

Blood wells up from the cut. She gathers some with her fingers, licks it off, her eyes closed as if she's savoring the taste. "Lovely," she murmurs. "Truly delicious."

She rocks back and forth on his cock, wringing choked groans from Jeremy's throat. "Magnificent," she sighs. Her daggerlike nails open a wound across his right breast. This one is deeper, and bleeds more. Mai bends to lap hungrily at the red fountain. At the same time she pumps him with her pussy, writhing on top of him.

The more blood she drinks, the more excited she becomes. Her nails flash across Jeremy's torso, carving bloody furrows into his fair skin. Her mouth sucks the ruddy fluid that trickles from a gash near his collarbone. She licks up the gore that pools in his navel. All the while she is bouncing on his obviously still hard cock, moaning and twisting, grinding her pelvis against him.

Then she stops suddenly, breathing hard, her alabaster breasts damp with sweat. "But I should save something for poor Harry, shouldn't I? You can come, though, little one." She arches back, and Jeremy yells, again and again. She is milking him, pulling the come from his body. At the same time, she slashes her lethal nails across his throat.

She rises from his twitching body, bends and laps at his bleeding throat. He is still alive. The wound is not that deep. His penis jerks and shudders as she drinks, still hard. Still aroused by her irresistible allure.

"That's enough for you, for now. I don't want to use you up all at once." She turns to me, her black eyes gleaming. "Now, Harry, what about you?" She kneels between my spread thighs. "Are you ready for some fun?"

I should scream. I should fight her. I should be too frightened to be aroused. My cock should be limp with terror like the rest of me.

I'm hard as granite.

Mai mounts me, her painted lips inches from my cock, her pussy hovering above my face. The scent of her is overpowering, rank and dark. She crouches, brushing her silky black bush across my lips. At the same time, she sweeps her tongue around the helmet of my cock.

I arch up, trying to work my cock into her mouth. She laughs, a sweet melody that makes me completely forget my bleeding friend lying beside me.

"Yum. You're so eager! You want a good time, too, don't you?" She reaches down to open her cleft and lowers herself to me. "Have a taste, Harry." I take a deep breath as her pussy settles on my face.

I lap at her blindly, running my tongue up and down her folds. Her slick folds are unexpectedly cool. Her juices taste salty and metallic, unlike any other woman I've ever eaten. I don't care, not at all. Every sensation, smell, taste, touch, inflames me further. I find her clit, a glowing bead of heat hiding in that chill dampness. I stab at it with my tongue. She jerks above me, grinding against the hardness of my jaw. I suck on the hot little nodule, sensing her growing excitement. I graze it with my teeth and Mai gives a delighted cry, writhing against my lips.

"Oh, darling! Oh, yes!" All at once my cock is drowned in the steaming wetness of her mouth. I don't know what she's doing but I've never felt anything like it. Suction, pressure, a rhythmic pumping that draws the juice up from my balls and into my shaft. I'll come in an instant, I think with regret, and then it will be over.

Pain pulls me back from the brink. Something stabs the inside of my thigh, then slices upward toward my scrotum. Her cunt muffles my scream. She releases my cock from her inhumanly talented mouth. Her searing tongue lapping at the wound feels equally exquisite. She pricks my other thigh, opens my flesh, and drinks. Her tongue soothes and excites me simultaneously. She pumps my cock with her hand as she licks up the fluid oozing from my torn body, bringing me to the edge once again.

Her daggerlike nail cuts a path along my shaft. Her mouth returns to my cock, sliding up and down, smearing and swallowing the blood that I feel anointing my organ. My cock throbs; my heart pounds in time. I relax and give myself to her. It's not pain anymore. It is insane, unbearable, impossible pleasure.

Drowned in her scent, I float in a rosy sea of lust. My balls are huge and heavy. My cock is a stone pillar. I feel weak as a newborn. All my strength has rushed to that rod of flesh where my lover is feeding.

Dimly, I hear a choking sound. Mai whirls around until her face hovers above mine. Her cheeks are smeared with my blood. Her eyes blaze in her gorgeous pale face. "I've got to fuck you,

Harry," she cries. "I can't wait any longer."

She slams her pussy down onto my cock. Ice races through my veins first, then searing heat. Her cunt muscles clench around my flesh like a steel vise. My wounds ache and sting. I barely notice. My cock swells inside her. I try to thrust but she holds me down, squeezing until I think my over-inflated organ will burst from the pressure.

Mai grips my shoulders, riding me with awful abandon. She impales herself on me again and again. The blood flows. Her hair is wild and tangled around her face. Her demon's eyes are closed, her teeth bared, as she strains for release.

"Argh!" She gives a strangled cry and convulses around my cock. Pain surges for a moment and I nearly black out. The pain shatters whatever was holding me back from coming. Semen boils up my stalk and erupts inside her. She falls forward onto my chest as climax takes her, ripping two red trails down my torso as she falls into a kind of stupor.

Gradually my heart slows. My breathing returns to normal. Squirming in my bonds, I manage to roll her inert body off mine. She lies on the bed between Jeremy and me. Her perfect beauty is hardly marred by the traces of gore on her alabaster cheeks. Despite my exhaustion and pain, I feel my cock begin to rise again.

Her long lashes flutter, her eyes half-open. She catches me staring at her and smiles. "Ah, Harry! That was so lovely. *Sanuk maak*. But coming makes me so sleepy…. I need to sleep for a little while. We'll play again soon. You're both still very much alive, and it's a long time until dawn…."

She sinks back into a state of insensibility, her graceful limbs relaxed and loose on top of the stained sheets. I lie there watching her, growing more aroused by the moment. Her delicate thighs are streaked with red. I feel the stickiness in my groin, the wetness that I know does not come from our sex. My cock continues to stiffen.

Logic tells me that I should try to escape, now when she is sated and unconscious. I'm fairly sure there must be a way to unfasten these cuffs. I may not have much time. I should free myself, grab Jeremy, and get the hell out of here while I have the chance.

I can't move, though. I don't want to move. All I want to do is stare at her unearthly beauty, wait for her to rise and take me again.

It doesn't make sense, but it doesn't surprise me, either. Here, in Mai's world, it seems as natural as breathing.

TURN

Nikki Magennis

He was at the barbecue, moving through the crowd as easily as if he'd been invited. Everybody was too polite to say anything. Besides, their attention seemed to slide off him after a moment or two, the way river water flows over a polished rock.

The smell of smoke and grilled meat hung in the air. Prue felt it on her skin, a greasy, slippery film that clung to her hair and fingers. She held a plate of food, but didn't eat anything. Instead, she took long, thirsty swallows of the red wine in her paper cup and watched him.

He leaned against the wall, and stayed there, almost motionless. Among the open-necked blue shirts and sun-bleached hair and candy-colored dresses and plastic sandals, he was a study in monochrome: black shoes, charcoal trousers, a crumpled white shirt with the sleeves rolled back to show his long, sinuous forearms.

"Like an undertaker on his day off," Serena, the hostess, muttered.

What fascinated Prue, though, was his face: unlined, so smooth it looked like a child's skin. His eyes were the clear, brilliant green of a swimming pool and twitched as his gaze flickered over the garden. Prue thought he might be smiling, but the expression didn't sit easily on him. His hair, cut short and severe, was pure white—a dazzling shock against that perfect tea brown skin.

"Well, he's giving me the shivers," Serena said, reaching down to slap at her bare ankle. "And the midges are driving me up the wall."

"Go inside," said Prue, waving her friend toward the open French doors.

"You coming?" Serena asked, tucking a strand of straw-blonde hair behind her ear.

Prue shook her head, already moving toward the man who stood at the edge of the gathering, apparently unbothered by biting flies or the sudden chill evening breeze. Sound dropped away as she neared him, conversations became brittle and shattered into the dark silence trapped in the trees overhead. All she could hear was the hiss of his breath—ragged, restless, and as slow as that of a dying man.

"Made up your mind?" he said, pushing himself from the wall and taking her wrist, as briskly as a nurse about to check her pulse. When he touched her, everything changed.

"Yes." The word jerked out of her mouth. Could it be that easy?

He leaned in to kiss her, a fast, rough kiss of the kind that sent her reeling. His teeth caught her bottom lip and the sharp buzz exploded all over her. She was elsewhere, suddenly, outside the world, and her blood ran hot and bold through her body. It reminded her of the time she'd drunk poitín from a bottle without a label—clear, vicious, volatile firewater that stung her eyes.

"You're not too attached, then," he said, pulling back and looking at her sharply with his chlorine green eyes. He slipped his hand into hers and walked with her out through the gate and into the alley behind the houses where the weeds peppered the dirt and litter washed up like flotsam at high tide.

"There's nothing here I want," Prue said, wondering where they would go, what it would be like, and how they managed to walk so fast without running.

The city streets melted under their feet, and it felt like she was in one of her flying dreams—free and distant and hugely, deliriously powerful. They flowed past cars, and Prue inhaled the dark perfume of petrol fumes. Far underneath them, she heard the scrape of rats' feet and the blind, hopeless chewing of earthworms burrowing in the soil. A plane passed overhead and she felt the point of its wing, as though she could reach up and flick it off course like a toy.

The moon hung in the dusk sky like a crumpled paper disk. The man looked up and muttered under his breath.

"Fuck. We need to hurry."

His hand was at her wrist like a cuff, and with every stride she felt the hunger of him, the sharp intent condensed into his body like compact muscle. He was built of desire, she understood; want was his fuel and his oxygen. When he took her, finally, it was going to be unreal, breathtaking.

Loud, drunk crowds on the pavement parted for them wordlessly. Neon flickered, reflected in his eyes and glowing through the pale spines of his hair.

"Where—"

"Quiet," he said. "From now on it's important you do exactly as I say."

"Okay," she said.

"Without question." His fingers locked around her arm

and squeezed so hard there would be bruises. She imagined the small purple flowers already blossoming on her skin—a tender bouquet.

"Can't I even ask your name?" she said, her voice almost swallowed up by city noise.

He turned to look at her, and the jade glitter of his eyes spilled over, catching something in her like sparks lighting tinder. It wasn't exactly fear that leaped in her stomach, but a larger feeling—the beginning of a terror that could tear a hole in the world.

"My name is Raam," he said, and his voice split in two as he spoke. "Aren't I the one you summoned?" He was laughing now, but his words were cracking and fracturing, as though he was speaking with many voices at once.

"Don't you recognize me, Prudence?"

Yes. Yes, she did.

About Raam there was a bitter, metallic smell that stung her nostrils. Her skin shrank and burned under his touch. Most of all she could sense a danger in him that answered the ache in her soul—or what was buried under the tiresome flicker of her human soul.

"I've wanted this for so long," she said, her voice grating.

He laughed at her. "You don't know what long is, my dear."

They turned the corner of the street where the lights were all red and the shop windows were covered with grilles. Raam spat on the ground.

"You'll understand everything," he said, "after tonight."

If Raam was destroyed, she thought, if his bones were ground to dust and his remains scattered in the ocean, there would still remain this—stain, a taint on the air.

They arrived at the small, nondescript hotel that Raam had chosen. It had to be somewhere anonymous, he said. Not

quite the gothic cathedral Prue had imagined—the lobby
was beige and slate and there were wilting lilies on the recep-
tion table. Prue, with her newly keen senses, could smell the
beeswax in the floor polish and the dried tears of the cleaning
woman, the stale gin-breath that had been trapped in the
surface as she rubbed at the dirt. Raam took the key and led
Prue upstairs.

The corridors were full of secret smells—businessmen's indis-
cretions that curled in the corners and clung to the doorknobs;
honeymooners' arguments that floated black and bitter around
the window frames, as if trying to escape.

The room was small and square, with a view of slate roofs and
TV antennas. A woman waited in it, looking bored and slightly
hostile. Prue smelled recent violence on her hands, washed-off
blood and the screams of a child.

"This is Nessa," Raam said, gesturing toward the dull, blue-
eyed woman. He removed his coat and rolled up his sleeves,
only a slight tightening of his mouth betraying any sign of impatience. Prue looked at the dark map of his veins and felt like
there were stars glittering inside her head, growing brighter and
harder every minute.

"Ready?" he asked. Prue bowed her head.

She knew what to do. She'd worn a white shirt, and unbuttoned the collar now, pulling it open between her breasts so that
Raam could see the shadows there.

He crossed the room with the speed of a hawk diving, and
took her face in his hands. He didn't ask any more questions—
they were beyond words and reason now.

Instead, he kissed her and the world stopped spinning. Prue
was no longer Prue; she was night and sea trenches, electricity
and magnets, blood and fire. Raam's mouth on hers was like
sucking a volcano, letting hot molten stone flow into her throat

and spread, leaping and burning, down to her center and her core, her cunt.

He was quick, stripping her of everything below the waist, tearing her clothes as though they were gossamer-thin flies' wings. She was flung on the bed, her legs splayed by his hands—fine-fingered and pale, but as strong as iron. Somewhere to the right of them, the girl called Nessa laughed, but the sound was a hollow echo caught on the edge of the tornado, and Prue was only aware of Raam's mouth, eating her now like a lion feasting. Freezing up, the terror a thrilling roar in her ears, Prue waited for the moment his teeth would pierce her.

She felt only the fierce licks of his tongue, lashing, digging inside and twisting in her, his fingers sliding into her arse and his voice a low growl that seemed to split the air. He was opening her, as one would pull apart a piece of fruit. His breath filled her cunt and seeped inside her, drenching her in the old hunger of centuries.

Prue wanted to scream, but no sound came out. There was a sound like bombs exploding, one after the other, continuously, and she realized it was her heartbeat. Or Raam's. They were merging, now, his force steadily overtaking her. She knew she was starting to turn.

He pulled himself up, climbed up her body and inserted his prick between her thighs. A prong like a beast's, blunt and short, shoved perfunctorily in her cunt, forcing her hips upward to meet it. Raam, who had looked so ethereal and strange by day, now showed his other face—the gleaming eyes and the hard snake-muscles of his body; his sweet, thin-lipped mouth gaping open, and the points of his teeth dotting the darkness. His hips were grinding against her now, his fucking both breaking and remaking her, the rhythm relentless, intent and devastating.

Prue struggled for a moment, her instincts kicking in—the

desire to throw this pretty monster from her, escape and find sweet, fresh air. She opened her eyes, suddenly, wide and violet-colored, and met his gaze.

Then all was lost.

When he bent his head to her throat, she tilted her head to the side. When his incisors dug into her flesh, she bit her own lips until they bled, and when he sucked at her, his haunches pumped slower and slower as he drew the blood from her veins and lost himself in this new, stronger lust. When he sucked at her she felt her mouth twist and she remembered what it felt like, in a way, to smile.

He came in utter silence, and as he did so she felt the new life flood her. It shook and coursed and crackled under her skin, sending explosive new messages across her synapses—something darker, too, a raw, exhilarating scrabble in her guts, a frenzy like a swarm of locusts clouding her mind.

She must eat. She couldn't wait.

And Raam took her chin and pointed her face toward the girl Nessa, looking wary now, scowling at them with a curled lip. Prue smelt the disappointment on her, the charred remains of a heart dry of hope, the thin, twisting desire that ran underneath.

"She wants it," Raam nodded. "As much as you wanted this, she wants—to be extinguished."

And Prue understood, as she took hold of the woman with her new strength, as she held her still and found the warm pulse point, how her acts could not really be called wrong, when the world was a cauldron of ambiguous wanting, of conflicts and confusion and lack and anger. As her teeth clenched down hard and broke the skin and she tasted the first sugar-wine blood on the tip of her tongue, Prue felt at last a kind of reckless peace.

CUTTER

Kristina Wright

Las Vegas: they don't call it Sin City for nothing. It's a city of garish lights and relentless decadence; a place where people go to gamble or get lost. The town reeks of foolish desperation and forbidden sex. You can't walk the street without bumping into a con man or a whore and you can't slip out to the alley for a smoke without running into a vampire.

That's how I met Kallinos.

The phrase "smoking will kill you" had never been more accurate, but I don't think that's quite what the health freaks mean. Of course, I didn't know Kallinos was a vampire. I took him for one of the rich players who are as ubiquitous in Vegas as neon lights. Vampires aren't real, anyway. Right? *Right.*

I was on my thirty-minute break from my job as a blackjack dealer at the Lucky Silver Casino—a third-rate gig, way, way off the strip. We—the casino girls—had been told to stay out of the alley. The threat of derelicts and rapists didn't scare me, but the mutant rats as big as raccoons did. Still, the alley was preferable to the street where I was likely to be mistaken for a hooker in my Lucky Silver getup of white blouse cut to show off my cleavage (sex sells—and it makes for lousy gamblers), silver micromini and white go-go boots. I didn't need a hassle from the drunks stumbling out of Lucky Silver. Not because I was above tricking—a girl's gotta do what a girl's gotta do, though I try to keep it legal—but because the drunks didn't have two pieces of silver to rub together anyway. I'll fuck for free if I know you and I'll turn a trick if times are desperate, but I don't fuck strangers for free. My morals may be loose, but they're my morals.

It was after eleven, but the August heat still hung heavy in the air. I rolled up the sleeves of my blouse for some relief, careful of the bandage on my left wrist. Leaning up against the grubby stucco wall, I took deep, productive drags off my third cigarette of the night. I kept an eye on the shadows in the event a rat decided my boots looked like cheese and moved in for a nibble. One minute I was alone in the alley blowing smoke rings toward a cloudy sky, the next...I wasn't.

I should have been startled. I should have moved into imme- diate woman-in-jeopardy defensive mode. I should have had the knife I keep tucked in my boot already in my hand before he had a chance to lay a hand on me. If nothing else, I should have screamed like a little girl in the hopes that someone inside the Lucky Silver—preferably Ja, our three-hundred-pound bouncer—would hear me.

I did none of those things.

I took another drag off my cigarette before flicking it toward one of the shadow-rats. "What's up?"

He was tall—over six feet—with the kind of dark, slicked- back hair I always equate with old-timey actors and George Clooney. His skin was pale, almost luminescent in the dark alley. He was dressed too good for the Lucky Silver, where the clientele is at home in jeans or polyester. It was clear he didn't belong here, in my territory. What was less obvious was where—exactly—he *did* belong.

He cocked his head at me like a dog trying to decipher human speech. He did look a bit like a dog; not a harmless Irish setter like I had when I was growing up, but one of those huge intimidating dogs—a wolfhound, maybe. Hellhound would be more accurate, though.

"You are alone," he said, his voice, thick with some accent, was like the brush of invisible cobwebs across my skin. "I am Kallinos."

His eyes had the look of a stoner—I couldn't make out any color in the irises. Either his eyes were nearly black or his pupils were dilated. I didn't know why it mattered, or why I couldn't look away.

"Yeah?" I scratched at my wrist. The bandage adhesive had been rubbing against my blouse all night and was coming loose. I hadn't noticed before, but now it was all I could do to let my arms drop carelessly to my sides. "What kind of name is Kallinos?"

"I am Greek," he said.

I nodded, as if I knew Greek from Spanish. "Oh."

"And your name?"

I felt like I was at an old-fashioned formal. I half expected him to bow. "Evelyn, but everyone calls me Evie."

He looked at my bandaged wrist and inhaled deeply. "You are bleeding, Evie."

Warning bells should have been blaring in my head. I should have been banging on the service door, which can't be opened from the outside. I should have been doing anything other than what I was doing. I was nodding.

"Yeah. Hurts like a sonofabitch, too." I scratched at the

adhesive again, noticing the dark blotch of blood through the white bandage. I was seeping again. Damn.

"Let me see."

I didn't even think twice about raising my arm for him to see my injury. He ripped the bandage off in one swift motion almost too quick for me to see and revealed the neat six-inch gash up my forearm. The wound had opened and was bleeding freely now. I took a step back, worried about getting blood on my clothes, but he held my wrist just below the wound. We looked like a couple frozen in some kind of dance move, him holding my fully extended arm between us.

"It is deep," he said.

I nodded ruefully. I probably needed stitches. Double damn. "I'd better get back inside," I said, though I made no move in that direction. "I need to rewrap it before my break is over."

"I can...make it better," he said, as if searching for the right words. "Help?"

"Are you a doctor?"

His laugh was deep, guttural. "In a manner of speaking," he said, his accent blurring the words. "But that is not how I mean."

I shrugged. "If you think you can help—"

Coherent speech became impossible as he raised my hand to his mouth and kissed my palm. I could feel the sharp edge of his teeth and I flinched, waiting for pain that never came. Instead, his tongue flicked velvety-soft against the edge of the gash. A ripple of something like arousal danced along my arm and I moaned. He lapped at the blood, dragging his mouth along the length of the wound. I whimpered, trembling in his grasp, and heard an answering growl.

"What are— What?" I gasped as he reached the bend of my arm and licked his way back down to my wrist.

He made what I could only presume to be a soothing sound in his throat but could very well have been the sound of him swallowing my blood. He sucked at my wrist before working his way back up my arm. I felt light-headed and couldn't seem to stop trembling. I gave a little squeak of resignation as my knees gave out, expecting to hit the ground hard, but he caught me, even while he kept his mouth pressed to the torn flesh of my arm. I wrapped my good arm around his neck and nuzzled my face against his collar as if we were lovers.

The feeling of arousal hadn't faded. If anything, it had only grown stronger. I became aware of a heaviness between my thighs and in my foggy state it took me a moment to realize what it was I was feeling: desire. I was hot and wet because this man—Kallinos—had licked my bloody arm.

Fear cut through the arousal and I jerked out of his arms. Or I tried to. He held me fast and I opened my mouth to scream, hoping to bring Ja running.

He pressed his mouth to my parted lips, swallowing my scream. I could hear the echo in my head. His mouth tasted salty, metallic, alive. He tasted like me. My pulse beat like a hummingbird as his tongue swept the inside of my mouth. I was repulsed. I was aroused. I was utterly lost.

"Why do you injure yourself?" he asked against my mouth.

My scream had trailed off to a moan. I jerked in his arms at his question, but there was nowhere for me to go. "What? I didn't—"

The lie died in my throat as I looked into those black, bottomless eyes. "It makes me feel better."

He nodded. "You carry pain here," he said, laying a hand over my racing heart. "So you transfer the pain to your body."

Hysterical laughter bubbled up inside me. "Are you a doctor or a therapist?"

He shrugged easily. "I am what you need."

"Let me go," I said, suddenly angry at what he'd gotten me to confess.

I didn't expect him to release me, but he did. I stumbled backward, still feeling like I'd just had the best sex of my life and needed a liter of electrolytes. I braced my bloody arm against the wall to steady myself.

Only it wasn't bloody anymore.

My stomach turned when I realized he had licked all of the blood off my arm. "What kind of freak are you?"

He spread his hands, encompassing me, the alley, the entire universe, it seemed. "I only wished to help."

"You licked my *blood*," I said, on the verge of hysteria. "How is that helping me?"

His voice was quiet, but commanding. "Look at your arm, Evie."

"What? Why?" I asked, even as I did as he said.

It was dark in the alley, but not so dark I shouldn't be able to see the gash in my arm. But there was no gash. Not only was the blood gone, but also the six-inch split in my skin. There appeared to be the faintest silvery scar in its place, but I couldn't even be sure of that.

I turned wide eyes on the stranger who had held me and licked my blood and somehow healed me.

"What did you do?" I asked, even though I could see with my own eyes what he had done.

"You were injured. Now you are not."

Heaven help me, my first thought was that I had found my new best friend. I'm a cutter—what else could I think? I trembled again, now with a newfound awareness of what Kallinos was capable of doing to me.

"You should be more careful. That was a deep injury, you

nicked a vein." His smile was predatory. "Not that I mind, of course. But had I not been here…"

"It was an accident," I whispered. "I don't usually go so deep. I know better."

I *did* know better. I knew where to cut and how deep to cut. I knew how to hide my wounds from friends and lovers, I knew which ointments would speed the healing and prevent infection. But this time…this time, the pain had been just too fucking much. I'd been drinking wine when the need to cut became unbearable and I had been careless.

He nodded. "You have other wounds."

"How do you know?"

Again, he inhaled deeply. "I can smell them."

I was pressed up against the wall as if held by invisible hands. Torn between fear and attraction, I was helpless under his steady gaze. I whimpered low in my throat—the sound of a wounded animal cornered by a predator. But sometimes the prey goes willingly to its death.

"Show me," he said.

With my back braced against the wall, I hiked up my skirt. I was trembling all over, my skin coated in a sheen of sweat. I exposed my thighs slowly—not because I was being coy, but because the nylon fabric of my skirt clung to my damp skin. He watched me, or at least I think he did. With those dark, impenetrable eyes, it was impossible to tell exactly where he was looking—until I showed him my cuts. Then it was as if every muscle in his body tensed, straining toward my self-inflicted wounds.

"May I?"

I wasn't sure what he was requesting—a closer look or another lick. Truth was, I didn't care. I wanted that feeling again. I nodded.

He closed the short distance between us and knelt in the gravel at my feet. It was incongruous, this tall, elegant-looking creature kneeling in front of me, an emotionally damaged black-jack dealer from a shitty little casino. But then he licked me, licked one of the many half-healed cuts along my thigh, and I quivered under his touch.

It was different this time, less intense. As if reading my mind—and hell, maybe he was—he looked up at me. The reflection from my sequined skirt sparkled on his pale skin. He looked otherworldly, beautiful.

"These are not so deep and nearly healed."

He sounded regretful and I felt like I needed to apologize. "I know. I told you I'm careful."

He nodded. "True. But I can heal them, as well, if you would like."

"Yes," I said, or tried to say. My throat was dry and any sound died on my lips as his mouth touched my skin.

My cuts ran up my thighs; short slices to assuage the pain. Two on the left thigh were from a week ago, when I woke from a nightmare about being pinned down and hurt; not a night-mare—an old memory. Another cut, this one on my right thigh, was just to tamp down the pain of being alone. He licked them all, slowly, sensually, and I felt the pain melt away. Tears slid down my cheeks, but I could not have said why I was crying. My body hummed with an ache that went deeper than the cuts he nursed—I needed more.

I slumped against the wall, knees bent, and a bystander would have thought he was going down on me. He *was*, in a way, but it was unlike anything I had ever felt. I pulled my skirt higher, over my hips. He yanked down my panties, my plain white cotton panties because I didn't have a man and wasn't looking to get laid, and suckled the cut that ran along the curve of my hip. This one wasn't as healed because of where it lay. Every time I sat down, the skin would separate and while it wasn't a deep cut, it was painful.

He laid one hand on my hip bone and one on the curve of my hip and stretched my skin. I felt a sharp sting of pain as the cut opened, followed immediately by the sweet relief of his tongue gliding along the injured flesh. My cunt flowed like a river—liquid heat streaking my thighs the way blood had streaked my arm.

"You are aroused," he said finally, licking his bottom lip as he looked up at me. "This excites you."

"I don't know. Maybe. It feels…strange." I felt drunk, having to talk slowly to be able to enunciate the words.

"I can show you a different—better—way to hurt."

A different—better—way to hurt. It should have sounded like a threat. To me, it sounded like a dream.

"How?" I whispered.

By way of answer, he cupped my bottom in his hands and raised me to his mouth. I spread for him, aching for the gentle swipe of his tongue up my wet slit. Instead, I felt agony as he sank his teeth into my thigh. I gasped, trying to fill my lungs with air to scream and unable to find my voice. It was like no pain I had ever inflicted upon myself; it felt as if his teeth went to the bone. I gripped his hair, twisting the slick strands between my fingers, at odds between pushing him away and pulling him closer. I settled on a strange push-pull motion, which seemed to ease the pain slightly.

Then, as sudden as the initial onslaught, came the exquisite pleasure—not orgasm, but close. I heard myself moan as if from a great distance, felt him sucking at the wound he had created and leaving a pleasant feeling of euphoria behind. I closed my eyes as my world shrank to just this moment in time, this creature between my thighs.

He drank from my wound. I could feel the blood flowing from my body into him like an umbilical cord was connecting us. Surely it was my imagination, but I could feel his cock swelling—not because I was touching him there, but because it seemed as if I could feel the weight of it between my thighs, as if it were my own. I reached down, cupping first his cheek and then my own wet cunt, to assure myself that this out-of-body experience was in my mind only.

I laughed, euphoric in a way no drug could ever make me. He raised his head, his mouth slick with my blood. I was no longer repulsed—I felt as if I had been given an amazing gift.

"The blood force...it fills me," he said.

Whatever the connection the blood had given us, I knew what he meant. I knew he was engorged. "Fuck me," I moaned. "Now."

He surged up against me, forcing me to the wall and letting me feel his erection. There was no heartbeat in his chest, no rise and fall of his ribs as he took breaths, there was only this hard shaft pressing into my swollen cleft. He moved his hand between us, unfastening his pants as I pressed against him. He freed his cock and pressed it against me, hard and warm. I moaned, hooking my leg around his hip and reaching down to guide him inside me.

"Your wound still bleeds," he whispered against my hair. "I smell your arousal and your blood."

I nudged the head of his cock between my swollen lips. "You're hard—because of my blood?"

I felt him nod as he shoved into me. "Yes. You do this to me."

Each word was punctuated by a thrust of his cock. His blood-engorged cock. I gripped his wiry shoulders, feeling the light layer of muscle and skin over his bones. There was nothing to him, but his body kept me pinned to the wall, his cock thrusting into me with long, powerful strokes.

The bite on my thigh flowed blood. I could feel the warmth of it between us; smell the sweet metallic tang of it. My "blood force," as he called it: life. I imagined a puddle beneath us—my blood, my arousal—and thrust back against him hard. I wanted him to fuck the life from me.

He did just that.

I was on the razor's edge of orgasm when he pushed my hair away from my neck and sank his teeth into my tender flesh. I whimpered, though the pain wasn't nearly what it had been when he bit into my thigh. Then, as he sucked, I felt the ripples in my cunt begin, felt myself tighten around him as his cock swelled and pulsed inside me. As my blood flowed out of me and into him, I came.

"Kallinos!" I screamed, his name as sweet as blood on my lips.

He went still, holding me as I convulsed against him and screamed like a tortured thing. The ribbons of pain and pleasure tangled into the most exquisite kind of release. And then I felt my heart stop and his begin to beat.

The moment went on for an eternity and I felt myself losing consciousness. Then his tongue was on my neck, soothing and healing, and his cock was thrusting into me, hard and furious. I flopped against him, too weak to hold on. I felt his cock pulse inside me and distantly wondered if it was my blood he spurted back into my body. His moans were animalistic, perhaps terrifying, but I was already in the mouth of the beast and knew there was nothing more to fear.

I don't know when it happened, but my heart began to beat again. I gasped at the sudden sensation, so odd after the stillness, and fluttered my hands against his chest. There was no corresponding heartbeat. He was bringing me back to life.

"I will need to close the wound in your thigh," he whispered, in a bizarrely intimate tone.

"Yes, please," I gasped.

He slipped down my body and lapped at the wound while the world spun on its axis around me. I gripped his head, not in passion but in an attempt to keep from falling, as his mouth soothed the bite closed and healed the flesh. Slowly, I felt like I was coming back into myself, no longer connected to this strange man-beast. I wasn't sure I liked being myself again.

Too soon, he was standing in front of me, easing my skirt down over my hips. "You will feel better after a night's sleep. You should go home now."

I nodded, even though going home early meant being docked an entire night's pay. Right now, I would do anything this man said. The thought should have frightened me, but it didn't.

I could sense his impatience, as if his body hummed with a need to run, but I was reluctant to let him go.

"Will I see you again?" I asked, sounding like a coy teenager, desperate for the popular boy to call her.

His smile was again calculating, predatory. "Would you like to see me again, Evie? Would you like me to heal your wounds and give you new ones?"

"Yes," I breathed. "Oh, yes."

He was gone before I could focus on his retreating figure, but his words lingered in the still night air. "Then you will."

ONCE AN ADDICT...

A. D. R. Forte

If memory serves me right, and it always does except for things I choose to forget, there was a tree where I'd carved the image of a squirrel one lazy day. It should have been a fair distance from the castle, but not too far, a place where I used to lie on warm days and look out over the grounds, watching men in steel garments tramping with purpose back and forth before the gates, watching those of better fortune wearing silks and satin flutter by with no real purpose at all.

Not much has changed at all since then. I hope they haven't cut down my tree. I was fond of the squirrel. I'd told my lover the carving was for him, but in truth it was for myself, a connection with the wood, with the life in the tree. Carving it, touching it gave me a few moments of belonging, of much-relished peace.

I remember that time as one of excess, of too much emotion, too much thought. Too much hunger. I like to think I have grown in wisdom since.

There it is, a spreading old thing, when it had been little

better than a sapling then. All trace of my carving is gone, but I know the tree as well as if a sign hung about it. I smile and lean against the warm, living bark of the trunk. It is an odd feeling, leaning here, looking at the now-dingy walls of the castle across the green, the tourists milling about and taking pictures.

Sometimes I feel I can almost float between times, move within time as if it were water, if only I concentrate hard enough, but time is beyond even my control. The past cannot be changed—only atoned for, or fondly remembered.

I am here on a mission of atonement, or maybe it is a mission of kindness. I haven't had much patience for either in this existence, but as I've said, I like to think I've learned something of temperance. I shall see, I suppose.

The apartment is on the top floor, a loft. It would be a luxurious place, except for the musty air of neglect, the dust, the scattered things—books, papers. And permeating it all, just out of the reach of human senses, the smell of decayed life, of vitality and hope gone sour. It smells worse than any garbage or compost.

He isn't at home. I walk through the half-dark rooms, but there is so little to see: an unmade bed, a chair piled with unwashed clothes. The emptiness itself speaks volumes. In the shadow of a corner, I settle down to wait.

He stumbles in, collapses on the bed, groans. It's not a pleasant sound. Perhaps sober and alert some sense might prickle at his consciousness, make him turn to check over his shoulder, but as it is he has no inkling of my presence as I approach the bed. I wonder if it might not be a greater kindness to simply end his miserable life. Even blood like his, tainted with despair and addiction, is palatable enough. He's young and strong. Satisfy my hunger, end his pointless existence: why not?

I run my tongue along the tips of my teeth, feel the heat rise in my groin as it always does before the kill. I sit on the bed and run my hand very lightly through his sweat-soaked hair. He makes a stifled noise as I push his head into the pillow, then jerk it back and twist it to the side. With my free hand I yank his sweatshirt down to expose his neck and the vulnerable veins pulsing hard with pain and panic.

He scrabbles to gain control, to fight, survival instinct kicking in against the effect of the drugs. Because I want a look at his face, I let go, let him roll over before I put a hand on his chest to keep him prone. Eyes wild with fear and adrenaline, he kicks and twists, scratches at my hand, digging his nails into my flesh with the effort to free himself.

For a while we do this until he gives up, body and will exhausted. He half sobs and goes still, staring at me, not sure if I am just hallucination or bad dream. I want to tell him, he's not so lucky. Or maybe he's luckier than he realizes.

"I'm your angel of mercy," I say, laughing. I look at my hand, bleeding where he's torn the skin. He's no weakling this one, perhaps some old memory of warrior's blood still fills his veins. Now that the grimace of terror has left his face, I can see familiar lines, disturbingly familiar: the arch of his nostrils, the shape of his mouth, even the color of his eyes. Maybe fate is mocking me.

I sit back and let him go, but he makes no move to run, too drained, crashing from the high now. I know that feeling, I know it well. His eyelids flutter.

"Ah well. You get to live," I tell him, knowing the words are meaningless. But later I will remind him. I like to be thanked for my efforts, though heaven knows he'll hate me enough in the days to come. "Sleep well, wretched one."

* * *

He wakes late in the afternoon to find cold metal around his neck. I watch him explore the collar with his fingers, then the chain, fear filling his bloodshot eyes with each heartbeat. He tugs at the chain, making it clank against the headboard of the bed, realizing that it's secured to the foot and he isn't going anywhere. That's when he looks around the room, seeking answers, and finds me instead.

Recognition spreads across his expression and he lunges before the chain and his own hangover jerk him back to reality. Retching and panting, he staggers against the bed, fails to land on it and sinks to the floor. He pulls ineffectively at the collar, trying to find the breath to talk. I'm more concerned that he will lose control of his bladder. I may be playing at savior, but I have no desire to nursemaid and he's in no condition to clean it up himself.

Crossing to the bed, I lift the corner and slide the chain out. I wrap the end around my hand and yank him to his feet. He stumbles along cursing and trying to resist as I drag him to the bathroom, but all he manages is bruised knees and ankles by the time I drop him before the toilet. I point at the bowl.

"Relieve yourself."

He stares at me, loathing and confusion and fear-fueled rage.

I sigh.

"If you piss your pants, I will kill you." Just in case he's forgotten last night, I grab the end of the chain and pull him to his feet. My forehead barely reaches as high as his chin. I slide my grasp along the chain to the ring where it links to the collar and I lift. He dangles for a few seconds, face going crimson as he kicks, gurgles, chokes.

When I let him down and put a steadying hand on his

shoulder, he has no problem unzipping his pants and emptying his bladder in double-quick time. I smile and pat his shoulder.

"Much better. I think we're going to get along quite well after all," I say.

I spend the first weeks watching him rage—at me, at himself, at the collar and the chain. I hunt only when hunger threatens my strength, and I can feel my own temper begin to fray at the edges from confinement and boredom.

I'm not a good nursemaid.

But soon enough chaos gives way to angry acceptance. His sickness abates as the pangs of craving lose their bite. I'm less tempted to wring his useless neck.

We settle into routines as creatures do when thrown together by circumstance. We adapt.

He cradles his head in his hands. We are sitting at the kitchen table, as we do on most evenings. I have one bare foot on the end of his chain as a precaution, and I'm reading a vampire novel. Urban fantasy, they call it. What they imagine us to be as we move among them. I chuckle, and he looks up.

"What?" he asks.

I read him the bit that's amused me, and he rolls his eyes. Winces.

"Why do you read that crap? Don't you find it insulting?"

I laugh. "Even the basest form of tribute is flattering." I shrug. "What can I say? I'm an egotist."

"You're a bloody sadistic bitch," he growls before putting his head down again.

"That too."

"Why are you even doing this?"

I put the book down and turn to lean my arms on the table.

He looks at me again. He's a little thinner than before, not that he had much fat to spare in the first place, and his skin is pale, as pale almost as my own. I put my forearm against his cheek to compare, and he flushes and jerks his head away.

I grin. Now that the worst of the withdrawal is over, his body is remembering how to live again. When I supervise his showers and his getting dressed, all with his collar still attached, he responds to my proximity, to my touch, to the sight of my body. It must be erotic for him after a fashion, the way I control every fact of his existence. The way I have stripped him of all façade and modesty as I've stripped him of his demons.

He's ranted at me, fought me, tried to reason with me. I've forced him, bullied him and listened to him. And so he has begun to love me—my violence and my power over him and my cold beauty—in the way victims love their captors. But he fights it with every inch of his willpower, resisting me at least in that...a good thing when it keeps his mind off the drugs his body craves.

"I have followed the fortunes of your family for a long time now," I say. "For centuries."

"Why?"

Here it is at last then. Unknowingly he wields one power over me, the power of ignorance. I knew I would have to answer his questions sooner or later and in so doing relive those hedonistic years ending in that sweet, blood-soaked, terrible moment. Maybe in a way, he's doing me a favor. It has been long and long since I have given confession.

I tell him simply. How I ran from passion to passion, seeking ever greater thrills, ever more debauchery. He nods, understanding all too well. I see the light of empathy in his gaze. I explain how I was changed from human to other, and how I reveled in the strength and bloodlust.

I tell him about my lover lying cold in my arms, eyes flut-tering as the last of life drained from him, and the whisper of shame in my own mind at my greed. It was loud enough to make me vow, even in my vicious vampiric infancy, that I would watch over what remained of my lover's slaughtered bloodline as long as I could, that I would try to redeem my honor if not my soul. In the end, honor is worth something.

His lips twist and he looks at the table.

"So I have a vampire godmother. Brilliant."

"You could at least feign gratitude."

He flushes and rattles the chain. "For what? This?" He drops the chain and looks at his arms. He rubs one scarred vein with his fingertip. "For this. Why did you even bother?"

I drum my fingers on the table and look at him, thinking.

"I almost did kill you the first night. I thought it would have been a kindness. But you remind me of him. And saving your ass has been more of a challenge anyway. I've told you, I'm an egotist."

He barely smiles. "I still think you're wasting your time. Demons aren't exorcised that easily."

I snort. "I'm the only demon you need worry about."

I've given him truth, but not all of it. I haven't told him that his blood will be more delectable when he's clean and healthy again—especially if he gives himself willingly to me. I haven't told him I'll enjoy seducing him, but I will.

I didn't think about this before, but it's a nice reward for my trouble. In fact, I think the effort will make me savor it all the more.

We find new routines. First I don't have to use the chain, then I don't have to rush through my hunt, then I start leaving him for days at a time, weeks. My wanderlust takes over, and I

disappear for a month or three. Yet I come back more often than
I've intended because I'm bored, and because my pet project
intrigues me.

One day I arrive to find him at the table with a half-finished
bottle of vodka. A neat pile of empty plastic bags sits in the
middle of table before him. He sees me and smiles.

"I flushed it all down the toilet," he tells me. "I bought it and
then I got back here and thought about what you'd do to me if
you found out." There's an edge to his smile as he pours another
shot of vodka and raises the glass.

"Here's to you vampire godmother. Well done."

I roll my eyes and leave him again. Longer this time. Six
months becomes a year, then nearly two.

I return finally on a clear winter afternoon. He turns as soon
as I enter the room although I haven't made a sound. I walk
up to look over his shoulder at the sketchpad, stark charcoal
lines on white. A winter landscape, harsh and unfeeling, but not
dead. It's surprisingly good.

"I decided to find a new hobby," he says, with his usual irony.
"I thought you would approve."

I lean on the windowsill, glad that clouds block the weak
sunlight.

"I do approve. I would compliment your talent but you
already know it's good."

He nods. "Yes. I know it is."

I watch the movement of his body under his T-shirt as he
rises and comes to stand before me. I smell his strength and his
lust, and I run my tongue along my teeth.

He reaches out and hesitates just a moment at the neck of
my dress. I look at him, motionless. He smiles, no sarcasm this
time, just male lust, and I watch him rip the material apart,
baring my breasts. I watch his hands cup them. He traces the

light blue veins under the skin and strokes the pale brown tips of my nipples.

His mouth is fiercely hot when he kisses me. His tongue fires the blood lust in my stomach and my groin. After he strips the dress from me, I return the favor with his T-shirt so that I can run my hands over his naked skin and feel the blood pulsing under it.

I feel it flowing into his hard cock as he fucks my cunt. Each thrust makes his heart beat faster. His sweat is salty-sweet on my tongue when I run it over the taut muscle of his shoulder, the line of his jaw, the arch of his neck.

Oh gods above and below, his neck, the fragile barrier of his skin, fragrant with perspiration and cologne, moving under my trembling mouth: so hot, so perfect. I whimper with frustrated desire, and he grips my ass harder, thrusts harder. Pushing himself to the peak before my self-control gives out. I slide my arms around his back, press my cheek to the crook of his shoulder. I'm shaking with my need, but I won't ruin my own feast, not when I've waited and cultivated it for so long.

He's almost there. His thrusts knock the wind from his body, his nails break my skin, making it bleed, sending slivers of pain through my bloodlust-addled mind. He pulls back and I look at his face. I see his hunger, his desperation, his need for this ecstasy.

I drag his head down and my mouth closes over his flesh again. I pierce the carotid artery and I feel him jerk, hear him cry out. I taste my first mouthful of his blood as he comes.

For the first time in centuries, my preternatural heart falters in its ponderous, inexorable rhythm. My body shudders. I moan even as I swallow.

Gods, it is sweeter, more succulent, more tart, more savory than any taste I have ever known. Each mouthful is agonizing

pleasure: such luscious pleasure, such spasms of delight. I close
my eyes and arch my body against his, and as my cunt tightens
around his cock, he spasms again. His heart sends another shot
of orgasm-rich blood to my waiting tongue. I savor it.

I never want to drink anything but this.

But he's faltering now, weakening. His heart beats slower
now, almost matching my own. It will stop if I don't.

I twist my head away and clamp my lips shut against greed. I
press my thumb against the tiny wound on his neck to stanch the
blood flow, and his weight sags heavy in my arms. His breathing
is uneven, and his skin cold, but I take him to the bed and stuff
him under the covers. He will live. Again.

Because I crave the taste of that blood. His blood.

Like a drug.

Our routines, our rituals change once more. I roam to hunt,
but I return to the den when I am done. I make him wait until
I see the desperation in his eyes, until he fidgets and swears and
cannot sit still.

Then I let him fuck me, in whatever way he desires, for hours
that seem endless. My body is tireless and the pain he inflicts
is only spice to my hunger. The bruises he leaves fade within
minutes, the welts within hours.

I force him to come when I've had enough.

And he lets me drink. A bit at a time, from his wrist or his
thigh or some part of his body where I've torn the skin. There
isn't much of his body I haven't violated, but then, there's little
of mine he hasn't used in turn.

I catch sight of us sometimes in mirrors, once with him behind
me, his cock tight in my ass, and his bleeding wrist pressed to my
mouth, our eyes glazed with euphoria, with the high.

Such is the unspeakable symbiosis that is our existence.

Sometimes I even let him pat me on the head, tolerating the insolence because I know it is his way of saying thanks for his life, for my help. I'm fond of him, and I know now why I let him live, why I paused that very first night.

His face doesn't remind me of my lover's. Not with its hunger, its restlessness, the need to find an ever better height from which to fall, the eternal search for the high. No. It reminds me of my own.

Ah, what can I say? I'm an egotist.

ABOUT THE AUTHORS

LISETTE ASHTON (www.lisetteashton.co.uk) is a U.K. author who has published more than two dozen erotic novels and countless short stories. Written principally for Virgin's Nexus imprint, Lisette's stories have been described by reviewers as "no-holds-barred naughtiness" and "good dirty fun."

MICHELLE BELANGER (www.michellebelanger.com) is an author best known for her nonfiction works on vampires. You may have seen her in a documentary or two. With the publication of her first novel, *This Heart of Flame*, her supernatural fiction has also begun to gain recognition.

ANNA BLACK is published in *The MILF Anthology*, *Cowboy Lover: Erotic Tales of the Wild West*, Zane's *Purple Panties* and *Honey Flava*, *Hurts So Good* and *The Mammoth Book of the Kama Sutra*. She writes for Ellora's Cave under the name Jenna Reynolds. Find both her and Jenna at www.jennareynolds.com.

KATHLEEN BRADEAN's (KathleenBradean.blogspot.com) stories can be found in *Where the Girls Are*, *Coming Together: Against the Odds* and *Best Women's Erotica 2007*, to name a few. Her reviews can be found online at Erotica Revealed and The Erotica Readers and Writers Association.

ANDREA DALE's (www.cyvarwydd.com) stories have appeared in *Bottoms Up, Frenzy* and *Do Not Disturb,* among others. With coauthors, she has sold novels *A Little Night Music* (Sarah Dale) and *Cat Scratch Fever* (Sophie Mouette) and even more stories. Her favorite vampires are Spike and George Hamilton's Dracula.

CIARA FINN lives in the United Kingdom with a partner, a laptop, her libido, and too many books. Outside of fiction she writes on topics from sexuality to sewing. She is currently torn between far too many novel ideas, and is considering the merits of a career in literary deviance.

A. D. R. FORTE's (www.adrforte.com) erotic short fiction appears in various anthologies including *Best Women's Erotica 2008, Hurts So Good* and *Where the Girls Are* from Cleis Press. Her stories have also been featured in several *Black Lace: Wicked Words* collections.

AMBER HIPPLE (www.myspace.com/amberhipple) is a frazzled Texan who writes about intense emotions when she finds time between working, crocheting, a demanding cat, reading, video games, and a long-distance relationship. Her hobbies include collapsing from sheer exhaustion, eating over the sink, and bubble baths.

MAXIM JAKUBOWSKI is a British writer, editor and publisher, responsible for fifteen volumes of the *Mammoth Book of Erotica* series. His last novel is *Confessions of a Romantic Pornographer.* Once described as the "King of the Erotic Thriller" by *The Times,* he is not even aware of his blood group, nor has he a website.

G. B. KENSINGTON has always been fascinated with things that go bump in the night and loves to tell stories that make you afraid to turn off the lights. Visit http://letters2charlie.blogspot. com the next time you're out after dark. She won't leave a light on for you.

NIKKI MAGENNIS is the author of two erotic novels, *Circus Excite* and *The New Rakes*, published by Black Lace. Her short stories can be found in anthologies including *The Mammoth Book of Best New Erotica Volumes 7* and *8, Hurts So Good* and *J Is for Jealousy*.

Prolific author of hundreds of dirty tales and ringleader of the Blow Hard Tour 2009, **SOMMER MARSDEN's** (SmutGirl. blogspot.com) anthology *Lucky 13* was released in April 2009. Sommer lives in Maryland where you might spot her drinking red wine or running. But not simultaneously.

EVAN MORA is a recovering corporate banker living in Toronto who's thrilled to put pen to paper after years of daydreaming in boardrooms. Her work can be found in *Best Lesbian Erotica '09, Best Lesbian Romance '09* and *Where the Girls Are.*

MADELEINE OH (www.madelineoh.com) is a transplanted Brit, retired LD teacher, and grandmother now living in Ohio with her husband of thirty-eight years. She has also sold erotica to Ellora's Cave, Changeling Press, Phaze, Black Lace, Samhain Publishing and many magazines and anthologies.

REMITTANCE GIRL (www.remittancegirl.com) lives in exile in Vietnam, growing orchids and writing erotica. Her stories have been featured in a number of anthologies including *M.*

Christian and Sage Vivant's *Garden of the Perverse* and Lisabet Sarai's *Cream*.

TERESA NOELLE ROBERTS (teresanoelleroberts.com) has stories in *Best Women's Erotica*, *Hurts So Good*, *Spanked: Red-Cheeked Erotica*, *Dirty Girls*, and many similar mother-embarrassing titles. Her first erotic romance novel is due out in fall 2009. Teresa also writes erotica with a coauthor as Sophie Mouette.

THOMAS S. ROCHE's (www.thomasroche.com) many short stories in the fantasy, horror, crime and erotica genres have appeared in hundreds of print anthologies and many websites. His book projects include three volumes of the *Noirotica* series of erotic crime-noir, four books of fantasy-horror fiction, and three books of erotica.

LISABET SARAI (www.lisabetsarai.com) has published five erotic novels, including her new paranormal *Serpent's Kiss* and her thriller *Exposure*, and two short-story collections. She also reviews erotica for The Erotica Readers and Writers Association and Erotica Revealed.

KRISTINA WRIGHT's (www.kristinawright.com) steamy erotic fiction has appeared in over seventy-five anthologies, including *Playing with Fire: Taboo Erotica*; *Dirty Girls: Erotica for Women* and five editions of *The Mammoth Book of Best New Erotica*.

ABOUT
THE EDITOR

D. L. KING publishes and edits the review site, Erotica Revealed and is the author of two novels, *The Melinoe Project* and *The Art of Melinoe*. Her short stories can be found most recently in *Swing!, Girl Crazy, The Mammoth Book of Best New Erotica '08, Best Women's Erotica '09, Best Lesbian Erotica '08, Frenzy, Yes, Ma'am,* and *Yes, Sir*. In addition to *The Sweetest Kiss: Ravishing Vampire Erotica*, she has also edited *Where the Girls Are: Urban Lesbian Erotica* for Cleis Press. Find her at dlkingerotica.com.